TEA WITH MR. ROCHESTER

FRANCES TOWERS was born in 1885 in Calcutta, where her father was a British government official. From age nine she was schooled in Britain. At nineteen she began in a clerical post at the Bank of England, making lively contributions to its house magazine until her resignation in 1933. Towers never wrote full-time, but produced stories, articles, and competition entries in the interstices of paid work, indulging there too her other passions, professedly 'for Gothic architecture, Old Masters and mountains'. Towers's first short story was published in 1929, when she was forty-four years old. Her work appeared most often in publications of a genteel ilk: *The Queen* magazine in Britain and, in the U.S., *Ladies' Home Journal*. In the late 1930s Towers took up a teaching post at a girls' boarding school in Harrow, where her sister was headmistress. Most of the stories included in this, her only collection, were written in the 1940s, while she taught English and History there. She died, suddenly from pneumonia, on New Year's Day, 1948, aged sixty-three. *Tea With Mr. Rochester* was published the following year.

ALICE FERREBE is Head of Academic Skills at the University of Chester. She is the author of *Masculinity in Male-Authored Fiction, 1950-2000* (Palgrave Macmillan, 2005) and *Literature of the 1950s: Good, Brave Causes* (Edinburgh University Press, 2012). She is currently writing a book on the writer Elizabeth Taylor.

FRANCES TOWERS

Tea with Mr. Rochester

and other stories

With a new introduction by
ALICE FERREBE

VALANCOURT BOOKS

Tea with Mr. Rochester and Other Stories by Frances Towers
First published in the United Kingdom by Michael Joseph in 1949
First American edition published by Valancourt Books in 2024

Published by Valancourt Books, Richmond, Virginia
http://www.valancourtbooks.com

ISBN 978-1-960241-12-2 (paperback)
Also available as an electronic book.

Cover illustration by M. S. Corley, design by Valancourt Books
Set in Dante MT

CONTENTS

INTRODUCTION

'I was brought up a child of light', begins one of Frances Towers' young narrators. The author herself was born into the haze of Calcutta in 1885, the eldest of five children of a British Government telegraph engineer and the daughter of a soldier in the Indian army. From age nine Frances was schooled in Britain. At nineteen she began in a clerical post at the Bank of England, making obtrusively lively contributions to its austere house magazine, until her resignation in 1933. Towers never wrote full-time, but produced stories, articles, and competition entries in the interstices of paid work, indulging there too her other passions, professedly 'for Gothic architecture, Old Masters and mountains'.[1] Towers' first short story was published in 1929, when she was forty-four years old. Her work appeared most often in publications of a genteel ilk: *The Queen* magazine in Britain and, in the U.S., *Ladies' Home Journal* ('QUITE BY ACCIDENT, PRISSY LEARNS HOW TO FLATTER A MAN', promises the latter publication's strapline to 'Tea with Mr. Rochester', unpromisingly[2]). In the late 1930s Towers took up a teaching post at a girls' boarding school in Harrow, where her sister was headmistress. Most of the stories included in this, her only collection, were written in the 1940s, while she taught English and History there. She died, suddenly from pneumonia, on New Year's Day, 1948, aged sixty-three. *Tea with Mr. Rochester* was published the following year.

'Her death', wrote Angus Wilson in his review of the collection in the *New Statesman* in 1949, 'may have robbed us of a figure of more than purely contemporary significance'. Even by British standards, this is rather mealy praise, but Wilson does warm to

1 Frances Thomas, 'Afterword', Frances Towers, *Tea with Mr. Rochester* (London: Persephone Books, 2014), p. 169.
2 *Ladies' Home Journal*, 1948 (65: 3), p. 41.

his topic. He goes on to commend Towers' 'subtle, allusive, but formal style', quoting liberally some of her best and funniest lines, and ending decisively that it is 'a bitter thought that we shall hear no more of this'. Wilson identifies a central figure of Towers' *oeuvre*, a 'little brown, humorous-eyed, plain, dowdy figure'. 'It is', he announces, 'the literary daughter', whom we as readers are urged to salute 'as one of the great manipulators of the English literary puppet-show'[3]. This persuasive creature— diminutive, peripheral, but powerful in her observational capacity and her wit—is certainly very prominent in the earlier stories. Prissy, in 'Tea with Mr. Rochester', is almost already parodic of the 'governessy' trope (a rare literary son, Lucas Silverthorn, uses this adjective to describe himself in a later story). 'One couldn't believe that reading *Jane Eyre* was wrong', Prissy exclaims. Initially, she shies rather prissily from the Brontëan darker recesses (the kind of thoughts discussed in her dormitory after lights-out), before revealing her hidden maturity in a sensual encounter when her Mr. Rochester makes her a gift of a shell.

Towers rewards the 'literary daughter' tendencies in her readers with an array of cultural references that are rarely obscure but always revealing. Research into paintings (Old Masters, mostly), poetry (Keats, most often, but Burns, and Herrick, importantly, too), fiction (*Jane Eyre,* of course), and music (Chopin, and Schumann) offers up small, studious insights into characters' sensibilities and relationships. Lisby, in 'The Little Willow', for example, is likened to 'the watching girl who holds a basket on her head in the background of El Greco's *Christ in the Temple*'. Towers' eyes, tellingly, were drawn to this figure, right on the periphery of the Old Master's view. But El Greco's girl has her eyes cast down, in fact, and is swathed not in brown (like a timorous literary daughter), but in vibrant blue and yellow. The shared palette of their clothing draws her, we might first think, into aesthetic and moral alignment with the disciple Peter in the foreground, shocked at the temple's desecration. And yet ... the basket of Lisby's double is capacious but empty, and her yellow shawl also matches the robe of the trader Jesus is attacking. Hasn't she, too,

3 Angus Wilson, review of *Tea with Mr. Rochester*, *New Statesman* 15 October 1949.

been making sales? She is—isn't she?—holding something in her hand. Could it be a piece of ill-gotten gold? Towers' peripheral innocent, this comparison prompts us to conclude, is a far more complex character than Angus Wilson implied.

Towers' gender, her reliably domestic subjects, her own assumed spinsterly gentility, all assign her work to a routinely critically condemned category—that of *feminine* literature. However, like an ingénue ruthlessly dissecting her society in a secret diary, the collection disrupts social expectations of femininity in an unusually uninhibited way for its time. A young girl dreading an engagement to bid goodnight to the guests at a dinner party cringingly envisages her own 'shivering, skinned-rabbit nakedness, thrust in upon their vinous warmth, their conviviality, their terrible grown-up patronage, in her skimpy tussore and black ribbed stockings, her sharp little elbows sticking out like pins and her arms all gooseflesh'. Towers' writerly matriline traces back to the unsaid ambiguities of Katherine Mansfield's writing, but forward too to the audacity of Angela Carter's work—indeed, Carter selected Towers' 'Violet' for her 1986 edited story collection *Wayward Girls and Wicked Women*. Like Carter's, Towers' many rooms have dark corners and supernatural shades. Of Violet, a servant, Carter observed that she is 'not averse to a little domestic witchery, verging—were her tale not told with such a light touch—towards the genuinely wicked'[4]. Violet is not Towers' only domestic witch (there is Miss Dellow in 'Don Juan and the Lily', and Mrs Asher in 'Spade Man from over the Water'), and 'Lucinda' is a surprising ghost story.

And like Carter's, Towers' writing is full of contrary taxonomies of women that insistently expand the representation of female experience beyond the tropes of conventional morality and sexuality. Towers stocks her stories full of flowers, meticulously classified and arranged in diverse botanical varieties of female characters—lilies, tulips, gardenias, zinnias, and blowsy roses. Her women are wonderfully strange and humorous creatures. Sophy, giving the thrillingly wicked Violet 'a quelling look', stalks 'out of the room with a giraffe-like dignity'. There

4 Angela Carter, 'Introduction', *Wayward Girls and Wicked Women* (London: Virago, 1994), p. xi.

are fish—queer fish—too. Elsa in 'Don Juan and the Lily' balks at the invitation to enter the bewitching Georgia Dellow's home, for it 'is one thing to watch enraptured an angel-fish going through its convolutions behind plate glass, and quite another to be asked to enter its tank'. Contrary to received expectations, Miss Dellow is revealed to be neither fish nor flesh. The story's Dark Lady is revealed as cultishly chaste. Instead, it is Elsa the sunny virgin whose propensity for sensuality is revealed. Gazing at Miss Dellow's hands, she imagines their boss, 'stooping his lips to take lumps of Turkish Delight from those curled fingers'. Sex itself is never again confronted as it is by a horrified Ursula in 'The Rose in the Picture', who witnesses her childhood beloved with his latest conquest, 'locked together and kissing each other … gobbling, as if they were starved'. Yet it is always here beneath the surface, sticky and tempting. Lady Hildegarde Pryde, in 'The Chosen and the Rejected', apparently an archetypal feminine invalid, reveals her love of a John Donne poem that recklessly 'makes one his mistress'. As Towers notes knowingly, 'the shadows cast by romance are stained with Tyrian dyes': that noble, classical colour purple was produced by the Phoenicians boiling sea snails in a deeply savoury stench. Towers' mostly young(ish) protagonists were written (mostly) in middle-age, and it is that queerness—that brew of innocence and knowledge, of romance and cynicism—that dissolves the traditional moral classifications.

As the stories accumulate, they become more and more concerned with the chiaroscuro—the light and shades of life, and their necessary co-existence in the best of people—and the best of art. In 'The Golden Rose', the pale Aunt Essie tackles her niece's horror at the physical component of love first with 'a scientific point of view, very cool and antiseptic', then emphasizes its ecstatic glory: 'with a spiritual legerdemain, she tossed it up to the sky and caught it again sprinkled with star-dust'. *Legerdemain*, meaning 'lightness of hand'—the term is appropriate for Towers' writerly touch, but also points to her prismatic work with light and colour. Like Sandra in 'Strings in Hollow Shells', we come to know, through these stories, 'people so rich in temperament that they seemed to cast pools of amethyst and sapphire at one's feet, like a rose-window'. Stories such as 'The Golden Rose' and

'The Chosen and The Rejected' turn on an understanding that beneath a bleached and conforming feminine purity lie the jewel-coloured passions with which girls become women: in Lucy Hill-ier's case, 'the red-gold woman of her most secret imagination'.

Décor and decorum—domestic goods and the Good—have always been closely linked, and Towers' closely documented, chiaroscuro interiors are moral as well as aesthetic spaces. In 'Violet', the furniture of the Titmus family home is imbued with ancestral heredity. It has 'that dumb but sentient look, as if something of their personalities had passed into it and fed and enriched it'. Georgia Dellow's witchy mystique is destroyed with a glimpse of her bedroom, like a 'dismantled old provincial theatre' with dolls and poorly tinted prints. Though Towers never set a story in the region of her birth and earliest years, the household placement of Oriental objects reliably signifies commendable taste and conduct. One story, 'The Little Willow', makes a Chinese jade its emotional and ethical centre. Towers' *objets* tend to have a striking radiance, even an agency. Lady Pryde's diamond ring, for example, seems 'to heliograph the intimation that she was a greatly cherished person, and to attract and hold all the light in the room'. In 'Tea with Mr. Rochester', as Prissy enters the home that is her Thornfield Hall, she notes of its furnishings that it was 'as if these inanimate things were possessed of a magical potency, endowed as in a fairy tale with a strange life and consciousness of their own'. Across the stories, lustrous bowls, tables and shells, like the flowers displayed with them, are strangely animated. They invite the trailing of fingers, they implore a caress. And when the protagonist of in 'Strings in Hollow Shells' touches her new lover's face, she does so as if he too were an *objet*: '"I can't believe it," said Sandra, touching his lips and eyes curiously with her fingers, as one touches a remote and haunting thing brought suddenly within one's reach.' All these domestic environments, simultaneously homely and strange, dappled with light and darkness and haunted by their pasts, are curated and presided over by women, for the domestic aesthetic, like the diary of the literary daughter, is a female art and a powerful dominion.

When a writer dies young, or rather, in Towers' case, early in their career, the work they leave is inevitably tinted with loss. But this collection needs no artificial colouring—it radiates light and life in an utterly unconventional cosmology of women and girls, light and dark, fish and flowers, and shining objects on lustrous surfaces.

ALICE FERREBE
University of Chester
February 2024

TEA WITH MR. ROCHESTER

The stories in this volume have previously appeared in literary periodicals and magazines on both sides of the Atlantic. The author, Frances Towers, died on New Year's Day 1948. One of her favourite poems, reprinted below, gives a better indication of her character than would any personal memoir.

She never found comfort
When a friend told her
To weep her pain away,
And offered a shoulder.

But a thin tan lizard
Lying on a boulder
Indifferent and delicate,
Greatly consoled her.

Marie de L. Welch
New Statesman, Nov. 2, 1929

Violet

THE only person Violet couldn't handle was the mistress herself. From the very first, Mrs. Titmus refused, in her obstinate way, to take to Violet; partly, perhaps, because Sophy had engaged her without taking up her references. So lazy of her, and dangerous. At her age, thought Mrs. Titmus, I could have done the work of this house and thought nothing of it. I would have been glad to do something useful. Utterly selfish, thought Mrs. Titmus, and bone-lazy, eager to grab at the first thing that offered to save herself a little effort.

But to Sophy, who had coped alone with the house for six weeks, it had become a monster that fed on the very marrow of her bones. So that Violet, stepping in and taking the reins in her absurdly small and fluttering hands, seemed like an angel of deliverance. From the beginning, the monster ate out of her hand. In less than no time it had resumed the orderly and polished look of former days. Skirtings acquired a dark glow, furniture a patina of port-wine richness, silver shone as if newly-minted. Any qualms that Sophy may have had that such a large house was too much for such a dot of a thing were quieted by her unruffled and competent air. But she had an effect in ways other than the merely physical.

It seemed to Sophy afterwards that it wasn't till Violet came to the house that the pattern of their lives emerged to her eyes. She was the focal point that related the different planes on which they lived to each other. She drew the design together, so that one became aware of values that had hitherto been submerged below the level of consciousness. With her smirks and the sudden gleam of light in her opaque eyes, her nods and becks, she illumined the hidden corners of their minds, she twitched aside curtains and revealed the fears and passions of their hearts, she smelt out their secrets, pounced on them and laid them out like dead mice, and she took a hand in their destinies.

On the first morning, when she brought the early tea into Sophy's room, in her neat pink dress with the turned-back white cuffs at the elbows, Sophy was aware of those dense black eyes taking in the rather tousled and puffy-eyed look which she knew only too well she presented on first awaking.

With an odd, humiliating feeling of being unworthy of the attentions of this crisp handmaid, she accepted the meticulously prepared tray.

'But you've given me the Queen Anne teapot,' she said, taken by surprise at the sight of this treasure reserved for guests of consequence.

'I like to be dainty first thing in the morning. It kind of sets the tone for the day,' said Violet, surprisingly. 'Madam's been down to see if I'd lighted the fire. When I saw her in her dressing-gown and her little plait sticking out, I didn't know she was the mistress. She fair frightened me. Must be nice to wake up in this room, miss, with flowers and that. They say you shouldn't sleep with flowers in the room; but I must say it's nice—ever so gentle and feminine. Makes you feel all glorious within, I expect. Madam said only toast for breakfast—is that right? But what about the master? Gentlemen like a couple of rashers and a fried egg. He looks a bit thin to me, kind of hungry-like. He was up ever so early catching slugs in the garden, and I took him out a cup of tea. He seemed ever so surprised. Poor old gentleman, ever so gentle and kind, he seemed. I think I'll do him a proper breakfast.'

'You must do as my mother says,' said Sophy, sipping her tea.

'Righty-ho!' Violet tripped out on her high heels.

But Sophy saw with dismay when she descended to breakfast that the girl had taken the law into her own hands.

Oh, dear! How tactless of her. And Mr. Titmus must needs make it worse.

'Ho, ho, ho! It looks as if I'm going to be spoilt.'

Mrs. Titmus looked down her nose. When her eyes had that pale, blind look, as if all the blue had been withdrawn from them, Sophy, expert at interpreting signs and portents, knew that trouble was brewing. Her sisters swallowed their coffee and fled to catch the 8.15 to London. They had their careers and were apt to shelve domestic problems.

'Someone,' said Mrs. Titmus, fixing the old gentleman with that glazed fishy look, 'seemed to be creaking about the house all night, pulling the plugs. I couldn't sleep a wink.'

Sophy began to chatter wildly about the news in the morning paper. The year was 1938.

'How silly you are, getting all worked up! You don't know a thing about it,' Mrs. Titmus said, with a venom that seemed quite unnecessary.

'Really, mother, I may be allowed to express an opinion, I suppose.'

'I don't know when,' said Mr. Titmus, seeking to throw oil on troubled waters, 'I've had a nicer breakfast.'

Was it possible, wondered Sophy, exasperated, that one so dense, so innocent, could have begotten her?

'I think there'll be war, and we shall all be blown to bits,' she said loudly and vindictively.

The prospect of war seemed a lesser calamity at the moment than the loss of Violet, which was probably imminent.

'Well, if we are, we are. It can't be helped, and there's nothing we can do about it,' said Mrs. Titmus, with the bored manner of one who wished to hear no more of a tiresome subject.

She rose and pushed back her chair.

'Ring the bell,' she said, 'for that girl to clear.'

'We must give her time to finish her own breakfast, poor little scrap,' remarked Mr. Titmus, genially.

There was a hideous pause. Mrs. Titmus stared at her husband, her eyes pale again with venom.

'What did you say? What term did you apply to the maid-of-all-work?'

'I know what father means, mother.' Sophy rushed in where no angel would have ventured so much as the tip of a toe. 'She really is the tiniest thing I've ever seen—like a little marmoset or something.'

'Well, I don't care for marmosets about *my* house,' was her mother's parting shot as she went out of the room.

'Dear, dear, dear! Your mother seems upset about something. You've not been cheeky to her, my dear, I hope. You girls are inclined to be cheeky, I've noticed.'

'Father,' said Sophy, 'you don't use a word like that about bitter females in their dim thirties.' She began to clear the breakfast plates with thin, nervous hands that shook a little.

'Now, what's the matter with her?' wondered Mr. Titmus. Deep in the recesses of his consciousness, he asked himself why one should have married a shrew and become the father of shrews.

'I don't like 'em, not one of 'em,' he said wickedly to himself in the dark depths of his being. 'This yaller girl, she's as nugly as an 'orse,' he thought, regarding her sorrowfully with his innocent, filmy blue eyes.

Oh, what an old dog he was in his deep inwardness! How ugly and vicious! He had a private atrocious language of his own, when things got too much for him, to express the exasperation that boiled within him. They thought he was old Father Christmas, did they? They thought he was a gentle old pet? Ho! Sometimes he was shocked at his own wickedness. Sometimes he was afraid of God's punishment. Suppose He were to take one of the girls! When little Beatrice had pneumonia, he couldn't eat or sleep, he couldn't keep his food down. If God did a thing like that, it could break his heart.

But sometimes he knew such flashes of glory, it was like the gates of Heaven opening. Suddenly a line of poetry would come into his head—or he would hear the strings of his heart playing *Sheep may safely graze,* and he would feel as light and holy as a sainted spirit.

He looked so wistful that Sophy had a twinge of conscience.

'Sorry, father. It's because I'm so tired. This undercurrent of drama all the time . . . Do you ever wish you were dead?'

'No, no!' said Mr. Titmus, shocked. *'With worms that are thy chambermaids,'* he said in a whisper, looking into vacancy, and stole away furtively, his shapeless slippers flapping at his heels.

Sophy's hands dropped to her sides. If she had opened a cupboard and found a grinning skeleton inside, she could hardly have felt more chilled.

'I couldn't help hearing what you said,' said Violet, suddenly appearing from nowhere with a tray in her hands. 'If you wish evil, miss, you attract it to you. It would be more sensible, excuse me, to wish to get married. One never knows,' she added, darkly. Her soft black eyes fastened on Sophy's face and clung there, like persistent bees. They were so jetty dark, you couldn't tell if there were compassion in them, or brazen impudence.

Sophy gave her a quelling look, and stalked out of the room with a giraffe-like dignity.

Seeking refuge a few days later from domestic tension, she went to her room and took a leather-bound book out of the bookcase. It was tooled in gold, with the title '*Morte D'Arthur* by Malory', and its pages were blank except for such as were covered by her small pointed script.

'Notre domestique,' wrote Sophy, in the green ink she affected, 'is no ordinary scullion. She might have washed up the wine-cups of the Borgias, or looked through the keyholes of the Medici. I have an idea that she can hear the mice scampering furtively behind the panels of our minds. I heard one the other day in an unaccustomed place. Father quoted Shakespeare and frightened me. I know now that he is a very lonely old man. La domestique knows it too. He loves his roses better than wife or daughters. It hurts him to have them picked by careless hands. Lalage is ruthless. She snips where she will and fills the vases. She comes into a room and stirs up flowers arranged by someone else, gritting her teeth, as though to say, How inartistic! What insensitiveness! She is a lazy, exquisite person, and, like a saint, exudes a delightful odour. It comes, of course, from a bottle and not from her bones; but is so much hers that the latter source seems the true one. She has the most charming hands and eyebrows, and is about the only person whose bath water one could use without distaste.

'I am deeply concerned about Bee. The other day a weddingring dropped out of her handbag. She swooped on it, and I pretended not to see. It was sinister, like finding a snake's eggs in a drawer and knowing that strange rustlings must have occurred while one slept. A mouse behind the panels. And yet her small, rather cynical, face is quite untroubled, and she laughs still in her silent, inward way. It's the secrecy that hurts, so furtive. And yet, what would you, in our household? V., I fear, has heard that mouse. "There's something about Miss Beatrice that calls to mind a divorced lady—ever so worldly and stylish. A woman of the world, miss, if you know what I mean. Now, if you was to wear one of her hats, why, you'd look ridiculous!"

'I told Bee and she went into one of her silent convulsions of laughter. "Poor old Sophy!" she said. "Mind you keep her on the right side of mother! Your face was beginning to look like an old leather bag." She meant it kindly.

'Does mother hate Violet for some deep, intuitive reason?

' "Lord, madam. I never did see so many pill-boxes and medicine bottles. Makes one think of hospitals and death. It doesn't do to dwell so much on one's health—makes the end come all the quicker, I daresay."

'I heard mother's voice, with an edge in it. "You can leave my room. I prefer to do it myself." She didn't prefer it, when I was doing all the housework. She preferred to write her lectures for the Women's Institute.'

Sophy closed her book and returned it to the shelf. In that household, with such a title, it was safe from prying eyes. It was her consolation, her other self.

Lalage and Beatrice drew Violet out and compared notes. She was a source of infinite amusement to them.

Violet's young man had thrown her over. 'That's all right. I'm not breaking me heart,' she said. 'It wasn't love, it was lusk.'

She cast a glance at a photograph on Lalage's mantelpiece.

'Excuse me, miss, but that gentleman's got ever such a nice face. I expect if he gives you flowers, they are real nice ones, gardenias and that. But he's not one to be kept dangling. He's got his pride. Never ask you twice, he wouldn't.' She sighed. 'I never had nothing from Bert, except a bit of dried heather he got off a gipsy. Mean he was. Everything for nothing was his motto. I suppose you'll be getting married, miss, before long?'

'What makes you think so?'

'Red hair and brown eyes, and then, your legs, miss . . . like champagne bottles. Miss Sophy, now, she's different. Only a very spiritual gentleman would single out Miss Sophy, and then he'd love her to the world's end. She's an acquired taste, as they say— and that kind's the most lasting.'

'The little devil,' said Sophy, when these remarks were

repeated to her, and for some reason she looked at the same time disconcerted and gratified.

Bee might have noticed it. Her small green eyes might have peeped out of their lashes with a piercing glint. 'Spiritual . . . aha! So that accounts for all these attendances at St. Petroc's.'

But Lalage was too lazy, too indifferent. One's heart might crack in two, and she would never guess.

It was a strange thing, but Christian Todmarsh did send her one day not gardenias, but orchids. She looked thoughtfully at his photograph. Yes, he had a proud face. He would easily be lost beyond recall. She rang him up, and their engagement was announced a few days later.

'Things always seem to happen when I come into a house,' remarked Violet, dropping her eyelids.

'The master and his roses,' she said one day, looking out of the window with a duster in her hand. 'It's as well to have a passion, even if it's only for flowers. My last gentleman had one for pictures. Ever so queer they were. You didn't hardly like to look at them. He said a thing I've never forgotten. He said there was some foreign painter that painted women as if they were roses, and roses as if they were women. That isn't a thing you'd be likely to forget. It makes a difference to your life . . . gives you ideas and that. Madam isn't a bit like a rose,' she added reflectively, almost under her breath; 'But Miss Lalage is. It comes out in her.'

Violet continued to skate blithely over thin ice. It seemed a shame that a gentleman with such a passion for roses should have no rose in his heart. Madam was like an east wind. She fair shrivelled one up. But she wasn't going to drive Violet away. So long as there were those that appreciated her, Violet would stay put. They needed her. Oh, but how desperately they needed her! How they had ever got on without her she didn't know.

She seemed to be moving all the time to some secret tune. Mrs. Titmus hated the way she laid the table, posturing and pirouetting like a ballet-dancer, setting down glasses and pepper-pots with a turn of the wrist, as though she were miming to unheard music, stepping back theatrically and regarding her handiwork with her head on one side, waiting for the next beat of the invisible baton. Even more irritating was it to hear her singing below stairs, in raucous abandonment to emotion, with that awful, vulgar scoop of the street singer who seeks to wring the heart.

But there were other and worse things.

'I don't like the girl, and I never shall,' said Mrs. Titmus. 'She pesters your father. I caught her taking him a cup of cocoa in the middle of the morning. He's so foolish that I've no doubt he drank it.'

'But what harm in that? She meant it kindly. She isn't a bad little thing,' said Sophy nervously, though she knew it was worse than useless to attempt palliation of Violet's offences.

'Nonsense! You girls are idiotic about her. She's *evil*. She's always *saying* things,' said Mrs. Titmus, with a pinched look about her mouth. 'Yesterday, she was putting clean sheets on my bed, and she said—"Look, madam, diamonds all down the middle fold." '

'Diamonds?' asked Sophy, blankly.

'Yes; the sheet had been badly folded, the way they do in this laundry, and there were little squares. I wouldn't have noticed them. "That means death," she said. I didn't like the look she gave me. If I were ill and alone, I wouldn't care to be at the mercy of that girl.'

Morbid, thought Sophy. It was a new aspect of her. Was there to be no end to the discoveries one made about one's nearest and dearest?

She looked at her mother as if she were seeing her for the first time. The thin face, hooked nose and Greek knot at the back of the head gave her the look of a teapot—was it? Or the Indian idol of massive brass that had stood on the hall table ever since she could remember, the head of Lakshmi, the goddess, brought back by some ancestor and bearing on her forehead the red seal of the Brahmin.

Teapot or goddess. She had something of both in her composition. She had comforted her children, and inspired them with fear. 'And now that one is middle-aged,' thought Sophy (who prided herself on facing unpleasant facts, to the extent of being guilty, more often than not, of overstatement) 'there is no longer need of comfort, but vestiges of the fear remain. I am still afraid sometimes that she can read my thoughts. I still tremble when her eyes go pale. This house, so shabby and so beautiful, is in part her creation, but she has long ceased to take any interest in it. She has become warped about money and won't spend a penny.'

Atmosphere is a mysterious thing. Like wall-papers superimposed to a thickness, maybe, of inches, atmosphere settles upon atmosphere with the succeeding tenants of an old house. The Titmus atmosphere, one felt (if one were a somewhat precious and fantastic creature like Sophy), owed something of its richness and duskiness to those others that it had absorbed since the days of Queen Anne. The sound of the harpsichord, she liked to think, had gone into the old wood. The scent of pomander balls was, perhaps, part of the peculiar Titmus smell ... faintly peppery, with a hint of Russian leather and petal dust, that clung about the house and permeated all their belongings and even stole out of parcels sent across the seas. All their selves had left slimy invisible trails. The furniture knew it. It had that dumb but sentient look, as if something of their personalities had passed into it and fed and enriched it. Was it too fantastic, Sophy wondered, to imagine that lately it had taken on a darker, stranger glow, a glint as of the reflection of soft black eyes?

One sound had certainly haunted the house since the day it was first built, the sound of the bells of St. Petroc's. They had a magical significance now for Sophy, like the aromatic poplars in the churchyard and the light that shone through the east window.

'The Vicar is in the drawing-room with Madam. But it's you he came to see, miss,' announced Violet, bursting in one afternoon when Sophy was communing with her book. Her heart turned over.

Violet fixed her with her soft black stare. There seemed to be the faintest trace of a smirk on her face.

'Did he ask for me?' enquired Sophy, turning away.

'Not to say, *asked,* but there are some things that are known without words. Madam doesn't go to his church, does she? Of course, this isn't his parish. You're St. Matthew's, reelly. He preaches lovely, I think. Ever so deep. The silver tea service, I suppose, miss? And I'll soon make some scones.'

Sophy went slowly down the stairs. If she had been summoned to meet an archangel she could hardly have felt more frightened, more inadequate. Never had she sought the acquaintance of this man who had been so much hers in dreams that she could not bear to face the bleakness of reality. She could not rid herself of the feeling that unwanted love is the basest kind of treachery towards the beloved. She had made herself free of his mind and his heart without his knowledge. How could he ever forgive her? She had created a world in which he was her lover because she could not help herself. But she knew that one breath of reality would blow her world to smithereens, and dash her to pieces. And yet there was a terrible, painful excitement in her heart.

'I am the Rose of Sharon and the lily of the valleys,' she said to her reflection in the dim Venetian mirror in the hall, speaking out of her dream-world. For surely it must still be a dream. It couldn't be that he had intruded into the real world in which one shook hands and took tea and made conversation.

The odd thing was that when she came into the room, Mr. Chandos's heart gave a sudden leap of recognition. A voice deep inside him said—'This is the face I have been waiting for. This is the woman for me.'

But Sophy as she looked into the bright pale eyes that were the colour of the sea, that were as cold as aquamarines, was thinking—'I shall not be able to endure the agony of loving this man.' The touch of his hand dulled her. There was something alien and terrifying in it, like the feel of a frog in her palm. Her mind felt cold and tingling, as though contact with the strange flesh of the beloved had frozen it. She rubbed it against the folds of her skirt, and still there was this queer, icy glow.

'Sophy,' thought Mrs. Titmus, 'is behaving like a fool. If one could only *teach* them.' For in her reveries, she was still the girl she had once been; another Lalage, but much more vivid and vivacious. Lalage would never know the triumphs that had been hers. She remembered that dress she wore that everyone raved about at the Hunt Ball that year. He had kissed her shoulder in the dark. She could never hear the *Invitation to the Valse* without remembering. What a lover he was! But she had lost him a long time ago. She never identified him with old Mr. Titmus, though they were one and the same person. It seemed strange that she should be married now to this old changeling. Once she had overheard him saying to himself in the bathroom— 'Now, where has she hidden my razor, the old ... *puss!*' So treacherous! She had been shocked to the heart.

She came to the rescue of her awkward, helpless child.

'My daughter says the singing at St. Petroc's is so beautiful. She is very musical, and has perfect pitch—which is quite uncommon, isn't it? So they tell me.'

Mr. Chandos smiled and looked at Sophy. He couldn't take his eyes off that face. It made a pattern that fascinated him, like a map of olden times with its 'Here are dragons,' and other strange indications. It was a unique face. New faces are seldom unfamiliar. They do not come upon us with a shock of strangeness, but are easily relegated to the different categories of faces which we draw up in our minds. Only out of history does a face sometimes look out with a hint of alien ineluctable charm. To Mr. Chandos, the face of Sophy Titmus had that quality. Her soft mouselike name enchanted him.

'You are not a communicant. I should have remembered you,' said Mr. Chandos, making a pyramid with the joined tips of his fingers and resting his chin upon them.

'No, no. I am a lost sheep. I came in one evening to hear the anthem, and then you preached; and you quoted Donne. And then I had to join your congregation. But how did you know?'

'A member of your household, Violet Wilson, told me.' (That girl! thought Mrs. Titmus with a little shiver as though a goose had walked over her grave, and thoughts of witchcraft came into the head of Sophy, already bemused and laid under a spell, so that her own voice, sounding out of the midst of the threefold circle that seemed to have been woven round her, was strange to her ears.) 'Did you like my sermon, Miss Titmus?'

'Have I not already told you? I see that priests have their vanities, like other artists.'

How hollow and far-away her voice sounded, like the voice of a stranger echoing in a cave.

A few weeks later, she was saying to herself amazedly—'I had no idea it was as easy as this. I had no idea. I had no idea.'

For the unimaginable had come to pass. He was no longer an archangel, but her own Paul.

She had thought everyone must know it when she came into the house, when she floated in with the moon in her hair. But when she looked in at the drawing-room door, no one seemed aware that something tremendous had happened. They were doing silly, unimportant things, poor earthbound wretches, and glanced at her indifferently with lacklustre eyes.

She retreated and caught Violet coming out of Mr. Titmus's study. She was carrying a tea-tray. The old gentleman had been treated to his wife's best china and the silver muffin-dish, which still contained what was left of the forbidden dripping-toast he enjoyed so much. A little posy of wild flowers in a wine-glass added to the general effect of festivity and loving-kindness. Violet was playing her favourite game of circumventing the mistress. She was watering the withered old heart. She was shedding the beams of love upon it and re-awakening it. She was queering the old cat's pitch.

'Poor old gentleman!' she said, with a sidelong glance. 'He does like a little attention.' She smirked self-righteously, and then, catching sight of Sophy's face, nearly dropped the tray.

'Oh, miss! Whatever is it? Your heart's desire come true, that's what it is! I'm *ever* so glad.'

There was a strange look of triumph on her face.

After all, it was her doing, thought Sophy.

'Things always seem to happen when I come into a house,' said Violet, *sotto voce*. And suddenly Sophy remembered a greasy pack of cards she had found when looking for something in a drawer in the kitchen.

'Do you play patience alone down here in the evenings?' she had asked, with a spasm of pity.

'Not me,' Violet had replied. 'They fall for me the way I want them. It's wonderful what they tell you, if you have the gift.'

Sophy was moved now to put an arm about the girl. 'I shall never forget that I owe it to you,' she said softly.

'That's all right, miss,' said Violet, dropping her eyelids. There was an inscrutable expression on her face, as if she knew what she knew.

'And now there's Miss Beatrice. But the cards don't come out right for her. Not yet, they don't. A married man, I should think, miss.'

'What do you mean? You mustn't say such things. I've never heard such nonsense!' said Sophy, deeply alarmed.

'Oh, it's all right, miss! You can trust me. I'm as secret as the grave.' And she disappeared through the baize door to her own quarters. To the ace of spades and the mice, thought Sophy, with a little shiver. Love, she thought, and Death, dealt out on the kitchen table by those small, clever hands.

So that, in a way, she was prepared for that frightening moment when Mrs. Titmus mounted the stairs to her room.

There was a look on her face, a sick and abject look, as if her pride had crumpled up in her, that hurt Sophy and shocked her.

She gave a backward look over her shoulder and closed the door furtively.

'Sophy,' she said, pitiably, in a strange whispering voice, 'that girl . . . I saw her. She was *pinching* diamonds into the table-cloth.'

'Oh, darling mother, she must go at once!' cried Sophy, flinging her arms round the gaunt figure.

For she knew now that Violet with a death-wish in her heart was about as safe to have in the house as a tame cheetah.

Tea with Mr. Rochester

School was an unpleasing Victorian building, the colour of carbolic disinfectant, with a pseudo tower perched on top of it, a shrubbery of laurels and rhododendrons, and asphalt tennis courts. Prissy knew she would hate it.

That first afternoon they had tea in Miss Pinsett's study, because Aunt Athene had brought Prissy, and she was not the kind of person to be sent away without tea. Nor was she the kind of person to pay Miss Pinsett the deference that Prissy felt was due to a headmistress. She put her elbows on the table and held her cup between both hands, not bothering at all to be gracious or to say anything clever. Her hair was done in two unfashionable gold shells over her ears and a veil floated from her absurd little hat. Miss Pinsett, in her grey coat and skirt and white frilled shirt, looked very neat, like a prim zinnia near an untidy rose. Their voices were different, too. Aunt Athene talked in a rose's voice, a yellow tea-rose's, and Miss Pinsett in a zinnia's, crisp and clipped.

Presently Aunt Athene put down her cup and wagged her left forefinger at Miss Pinsett.

'Not too many mathematics, Miss Pinsett, but as much music as possible. I think music is the most important thing in life.'

'But, shurly . . .' began Miss Pinsett.

'Yes, yes!' said Aunt Athene, 'when all else fails, there is still music. What consolation has algebra ever been to a broken heart?'

The diamond in her ring welled up with light that flashed like a star and fell as she moved her hand to adjust the little hat. There was a faint pink smudge on the tea-cup where her lips had touched it—Prissy hoped Miss Pinsett wouldn't notice—but the rock-cakes and the fish-paste sandwiches had been left undisturbed. Prissy was too miserable to eat, and Aunt Athene never did, anyway.

'Good-bye, *chérie*. You had better run away to the other girls now, while I talk to Miss Pinsett.'

'Shurly, shurly, Priscilla is not going to cry.'

Aunt Athene made a funny little face that said as plain as plain to Prissy, but not to Miss Pinsett—'Isn't she an old idiot?'

'Cry?' said Aunt Athene, raising her gold eyebrows. 'Prissy has Spanish blood. She is as proud as Lucifer, and as detached as . . . as a fish. Believe me, Miss Pinsett, I shouldn't care to look into the notebook marked "Private" that she sums us all up in. No doubt *you'll* figure in it, too. Oh! you'll have a chiel amang you taking notes.' She laughed her four glassy notes—so pretty, so heartless.

Aunt Athene had her own cruel way of being kind. She had saved the situation by making one quite thankful to see the back of her. How did she know about the notebook?

Miss Pinsett rang the bell and handed Prissy over to the school matron. It was the last she was to see for a long time of the study with its Axminster carpet and Medici prints and rows of encyclopædias.

Aunt Athene's gardenia scent seemed to follow her out into the hall.

'Was that lady your mother, dear?' asked Matron.

'My mother is dead. It was one of my aunts.'

'Aren't you a lucky girl to have an auntie with such luffly hair! Pure gyold!' bubbled Matron, wiping her mouth. Gush, thought Prissy. It made her feel as stiff as a poker . . . quite hard and cold.

Prissy discovered that one was too tired at school even to dream. No sooner was one's head on the pillow, no sooner, it seemed, had the gargling and hairbrushing ceased and the cubicle curtains been rattled back, than the rising-bell clanged rudely and noisily in the corridors. One's spine ached where it had bridged the sag in the middle of the mattress. A sharp peppermint smell of toothpaste in the dormitory mingled with the smell of burnt toast coming up from below.

But the worst thing was that there wasn't a moment of the day to play ball by oneself. She had 'played ball' ever since she was nine years old. She could not 'make up' without her ball. She needed solitude and secrecy and the rhythm of the ball's being bounced on a mossy path to spin out of herself an imaginary world and people it with characters as real as any of flesh and blood.

It was so safe (much safer than hours spent with pencil and paper, which might have led to inquiries); because no one could guess what was happening. If one came in looking rather pale and mad, with smudges under one's eyes, they might say one was a queer little fish and had been overdoing it out there alone in the garden, they might give one hot milk and send one to bed; but they couldn't *know*. Not even Aunt Athene, with her piercing look, could ever catch a glimpse of that other world.

All the same, said Prissy to herself, thinking of the holidays, one must watch out for Aunt Athene. It was queer about that notebook. Not that she would ever look at anything marked 'Private'. Oh, no! She was much too fastidious a person.

The notebook was a comparatively recent affair. It was a kind of a diary, really, and was concerned only with the real world. Somehow, Prissy knew that the things one just 'thought' and the things one 'made up' came from different parts of oneself. One thought with one's mind, but 'making up' came from so deep inside that one couldn't tell where.

'Thinking,' confided to one's diary and not to be seen by any *honest* mortal eye, gave one a delicious feeling of superiority. One was not so impotent as the grown-ups imagined. When one was sent out of the room on some improvised errand because of Mr. Pargeter's saying—'Little pitchers have long ears,' it was satisfactory to remember the entry—'Mr. P. is brown and squirmy. He is very like an earwig. If he was trod on, there would be a dark, oily smear and a bitter smell.'

There were poems in the diary, too. Prissy wished there were some way of finding out whether they were real poems. Aunt Elena, perhaps; but was her opinion worth having? Her favourite reading was a mouldy old book called *Urn Burial*, that she read in bed; and she liked creepy, rustling things like tortoises and cacti. She had a dark, haggard face that made one think of an old grave-yard, but her eyes were so dark and deep that when one talked to her, one talked *into* her eyes, the way one drops a pebble into a pool to watch for the ripples.

The mistresses and the girls were too ordinary for words, too dull to put into the diary. Only Miss Hornblower was a little different because she took the Shakespeare class, and one got the feeling now and again that she was keeping back something too precious to tell. 'You little owls, with your dull, stupid eyes!' she cried out once, her nose twitching with exasperation. She looked as if she were going to cry, and suddenly one saw that it was dreadful for her. She had really been in that wood near Athens, and now she had crashed into the classroom, and it was common and awful, and they were all common and awful, too.

Perhaps Miss Hornblower felt about Shakespeare as one felt about *Jane Eyre*, which one had extracted surreptitiously from the VIth Form library and read in secret under the flap of the desk.

What agony when the tea-bell clanged rudely and woke one up out of that dream! Gone were the vases of purple spar, the pale Parian mantelpiece. The master of Thornfield Hall had vanished, like the Devil through a trap-door. But, stumbling down the corridor, one still saw the flash of his dark eyes, heard the deep sardonic tones of his voice. Eating the thick hunks of bread and plum jam, one thought with anguish of the seed-cake Miss Temple took out of her drawer.

Towards the half-term a personality disengaged itself from the indeterminate background of moon-faces and pigtails to the extent of being half-confided in. Bunty Adams served as a very inadequate substitute for the ball game. The host of imaginary characters had retreated too far into the depths of Prissy's being to be recalled. Besides, they were not to be shared. One would as soon have said one's prayers aloud. Bunty was not even quite on the diary plane, but she was a receptive little thing and proved a rapt audience for the real-life dramas staged by Prissy, in which Aunt Elena and Aunt Athene played their parts, rather touched-up, rather twopence-coloured, as befitted creatures translated into the sphere of Art.

And then there was Mr. Considine. But Prissy did not speak of him, because gradually he had come to assume all the characteristics of Mr. Rochester, and Mr. Rochester belonged to that part of Prissy's experience which was too poignant to be shared. Her voice would go all trembly if she tried to tell Bunty about Thornfield Hall. "Jane, I've got a blow;—I've got a blow, Jane!"

Was ever a woman so honoured? He was so strong, so fascinating. And rather wicked, she supposed. For what was that queer business about Adele? Prissy felt rather wicked, too, as if she had a guilty secret to hide. Aunt Athene's eyes were so piercing, and she was so particular about what one read.

But she tried out a poem on Bunty, one day, in the dusk of the shrubbery, with the red electric trains clanking up to London beyond the iron railing. She read it in a thin, strangled, unnatural voice.

> I looked out of my window this morning
> And saw the hawthorns in bloom.
> When the golden day was just dawning,
> Their scent came into my room.
>
> They were white as the tents of the Arabs
> And humming with little brown bees,
> With dark little bees like scarabs,
> And my heart flew out to the trees.
>
> It is lulled in those bowers so airy
> By the incense-and-pepper smell
> That will make of my heart a fairy,
> Of my breast but a hollow shell.

'Oh, Prissy! I think it's super. If you hadn't told me, I could easily have thought it was Shelley or someone. I could, really.'

'Oh, no—not *Shelley!*' said Prissy, modestly. 'Of course I had to find a rhyme for "Arabs", and there *is* only one. You don't think it sounds dragged in?' she inquired, anxiously.

'Definitely, not. I think it's maharvellous.'

Oh, if only Bunty were a person of authority!

It was queer seeing Aunt Elena again, after all the things one had been saying about her; like meeting a person who had figured the night before in a vivid dream. She was waiting on the platform, in her old toque with the crushed wallflowers. Her kiss was like the peck of a hen; so perfunctory that it bereft one of affection.

But Aunt Athene at the front door, looking more like a rose than ever, drew one down into a secret garden of spices.

When one returned to No. 7 Queen Anne Terrace, it was like opening some old, adorable book and stepping between its covers. The wrought-iron gate had come from Spain. One looked through it into a paved courtyard, and there was the house, that looked so powdery one felt one could brush off the cedar-red bloom with one's fingers. The porch with its fluted columns, the shell under the fanlight, the blue front door and the tip-tilted windows were the frontispiece. Aunt Athene had come from inside the story to greet one.

You know those golden almonds of light that holy people have behind them in old pictures? Aunt Athene seemed to have one, too, like a person walking in beauty. Not that her light came from God. Oh, no! Her other world was certainly not Heaven.

'How funny everything looks! I'd forgotten it was like this,' said Prissy, looking about her. Everything was more beautiful even than she had remembered.

After the drabness of school, the drawing-room simply took one's breath away. It was pale, and patternless except for the star-tled silver deer on the curtains, and colours showed up in it as though spot-lit. The celadon bowls, the bowls of peach-blow and *sang-de-bœuf,* shone with a lustre that seemed to shed tinted pools of reflected light, and their delicate curves against the cream walls made one want to stroke them. The tea-kettle was bub-bling over a blue flame and there was a faint smell of methylated spirit and freesias, and a breath from Aunt Elena's greenhouse as of earth freshly watered.

The aunts asked innumerable questions, most of which were easy enough to answer. But now and again an oblique one came sideways from Aunt Athene.

'And is there any *talking* after lights out?'

One had always remembered two cryptic remarks let fall by some grown-up. 'There never was such a person for consuming her own smoke as Elena,' and 'Athene has such a beautiful mind.'

Aunt Athene had beautiful hair and a beautiful voice and beautiful laughter. Wasn't that enough? Must she also have a beautiful mind, to set her above other people and make her so fastidious that she wouldn't ever let one go to a cinema or read a book with love in it?

So, when she said in a casual kind of voice—'Is there any talking after lights out?' one knew what she meant. She meant—'Are there any *horrid* girls, who try to tell you things you shouldn't know.'

If she only knew how terrified one was of finding out about things one shouldn't know.

But one couldn't believe that reading *Jane Eyre* was wrong. And if it were, if at fourteen one had no right to have discovered so much about love, well, it couldn't be helped. It was the most thrilling, glorious, and beautiful thing in the world. It was like stained glass windows and sunsets and nightingales singing in the dark.

'Not much talking; we're too tired,' murmured Prissy, looking into her empty cup.

And suddenly she thought—'if she asks me what I've been reading, I shall get scarlet. And, please God, don't let them mention *him*—not just now, when I'm so tired.'

The holidays were haunted by Mr. Considine. There was always the delicious fear that one might meet him face to face. In a way, one wanted to more than anything in the world, but when there was a prospect of such a meeting, one was seized with panic.

Prissy had always known that he was a very special kind of person. When he came to tea in the old days, she used to have hers in the schoolroom. She remembered that his soft black hat on the hall table looked sootier and richer than other people's, his stick more unusual, his voice coming through the closed door sounded deeper and softer. And afterwards, when he had gone and one was permitted to return to grown-up society, it seemed as if something of his personality still lingered in the drawing-room, like the smell of incense in a Catholic church when the Mass is over—a faint tobacco and carnation scent. And the room looked different—kind of hushed and golden. More flowers than usual, the yellow fluted teacups, and a walnut cake. But perhaps it was Aunt Athene herself who seemed the most changed. The pupils of her eyes were so large they almost covered the iris, and she kept moving restlessly about and humming a tune as if she had just come in from a concert. Then she usually went to the piano and played the Brahms *Rhapsody* over and over again, as if she were continuing a conversation in her own mind.

One night during these holidays there was a dinner-party for some of the Cathedral clergy and their wives, Mr. Pargeter and Mr. Considine.

'I should think Prissy might come in for dessert,' said Aunt Elena, stalking in and stealing a salted almond from one of the silver shells.

Aunt Athene was laying the table herself, instructing Prissy in the art for when she should be grown-up.

Her arrangement looked sumptuous but careless like a banquet in a picture in the National Gallery; as if subtle and exquisite ladies with high, bald brows and bosoms of snow were to pose on the Hepplewhite chairs. The polished mahogany was a dark pool in which floated the reflections of pink, pointed cyclamens spilling out of a Venetian goblet, and iridescent bubbles of glass.

'A bit medieval, isn't it?' said Aunt Elena. She gave her little sniff, and there was a gleam in her dark eyes. That sudden gleam was what one loved her for, that goblin light in the graveyard. It was queer, the way she often echoed some vague, scarce-formulated thought in one's mind, making one feel that deep in her heart was the fire that would always warm one.

'Dinner with the Borgias,' she said. 'Alexis, and Simon P., perhaps. But what about the clergymen?'

'I think it's lovely,' said Prissy tremulously. 'But may I have my dessert in bed, please?'

For she could not, no, it was out of the question that she should be called upon to face the ordeal of adult quizzical eyes, *his* eyes, upon her awkwardness, her shivering, skinned-rabbit nakedness, thrust in upon their vinous warmth, their conviviality, their terrible grown-up patronage, in her skimpy tussore and black ribbed stockings, her sharp little elbows sticking out like pins and her arms all gooseflesh.

'Of course you can,' said Aunt Elena, hurriedly undoing the mischief she had done, while Aunt Athene's eyes travelled over her in a *distraite* fashion. 'Yes,' she said, 'yes. It wouldn't be very amusing for Prissy.' *Amusing*, thought Prissy, was hardly the word. It would be more thrilling, more frightful and perilous, than she could bear. Her dream world would be in mortal danger. She trembled to think what she might have to suffer if Aunt Athene were to catch a glimpse of it. Contempt, perhaps; or heartless tinkling laughter. She could imagine that Aunt Athene might even go to the lengths of telling him. 'You must know, Alexis, that Prissy has a crush on you.' The agony of it would kill her.

She had a few other narrow escapes, glimpses of his tall figure at the end of vistas, crossing a street, going into a shop. And then, towards the end of the holidays, the worst happened.

Aunt Athene announced that she was taking Prissy to have tea with Mr. Considine.

'But I don't want to go,' said Prissy, off her guard.

'You don't want to go? And why not, may I ask? When a most distinguished scholar has been so kind as to invite a little school-girl to tea, she should feel greatly honoured.'

Greatly honoured! But he hadn't asked her, of course. He scarcely knew she existed. Aunt Athene was taking her along as she might have taken a Pekinese or a sunshade. It was too much. She felt too young, too tender, for such an overwhelming experience. To meet one's hero in the flesh was terrible enough, but to meet him in the presence of Aunt Athene was an ordeal beyond one's powers of endurance. Those cool green eyes which missed nothing and dwelt with a faint disdain on schoolgirl blushes and gaucheries! Oh, God! make something happen to prevent it, Aunt Elena ... if only Aunt Elena could be substituted for that other one. But at the appointed hour, Aunt Athene set off in her lilac dress, her legs looking like glass through the thin silk of her stockings, with Prissy walking, cold with apprehension, beside her.

An elderly maid opened the door, and Aunt Athene stepped into the hall, her delicate scent floating in with her like some invisible attendant spirit.

Prissy felt very strange indeed. She felt as if the foundations of the visible world were shifting under her feet, as if the walls of reality were dissolving and those of the other world sliding into their place.

The pale April sunlight spilled into the hall and touched an old print in a maple frame, and winked in the topaz and agate knobs of a bundle of sticks in a copper jar. A bust of bronze stood in a niche, gazing out coldly into space. Prissy was so strung-up that she saw everything with unnatural distinctness, as if these inanimate things were possessed of a magical potency, endowed as in a fairy tale with a strange life and consciousness of their own. But what was Aunt Athene doing here, in this perilous place? If one met her in a dream, she was no more than a sprite, a quintessence of aunt, who was gone with just one look out of her green eyes, or a tinkle of laughter, or a key-word that woke one up, thinking—'That was most frightening and important.' For in dreams one sees only those physical attributes of a person which have served to express for one his essential being. But here, on the threshold of the imaginary world, she was too terribly her whole self, taking off her cape and adjusting the hairpins in the gold conches over her ears with those turned-back thumbs and double-jointed fingers that made her hands so speaking and theatrical. Her heels on the parquet floor went clickety-click, with the sharp little taps of a pony on a hard road. Her eyes were dark to-day, the pupils so dilated that there were only thin rings of green round them.

Aunt Athene followed the maid up the stairs and into a room on the first floor. A tall figure rose from the chair by the fire to greet her. Prissy hovered in the background. She had time to see, before Aunt Athene called attention to her presence, that this was not the drawing-room of snow and fire that had so captivated Jane, but a sombre book-lined room with chairs of red-and-gold leather. Then, as if she were crossing a vast stage into a pool of limelight, she came forward, stepping from Persian rug to rug, to take the hand held out to her. But he was still talking to Aunt Athene and shook hands with Prissy without looking at her. His hand was so cold, it gave one a fresh feeling, as of gathering snowdrops in a frosty wood. She stole a look at the face turned away from her. He wasn't so dark or so stern as she had remembered, and his eyes were blue, as blue as a sailor's. Prissy felt a little cheated; as one does, for instance, when someone in a book goes out at a door on the right, whereas in one's mind the door has been all the time on the left.

They were too much interested in their conversation to be aware of her for a long time. She sat on a slippery sofa with elegant golden feet, and drank in everything.

It was a very interesting conversation. Prissy tried to remember every word of it to record in her diary. She was very proud that a relation of hers could evoke the sudden delighted laughter that made Mr. Considine wrinkle up his eyes. She was proud of Aunt Athene's beauty, her wit, her tea-rose quality.

When tea came in, it would be terrible. They would have to draw her into their orbit. Perhaps she would make a noise gulping her tea.

The maid came in and set down a tray on a table in the corner. For some time they took no notice of it, but left the tea to get stewed in the silver teapot.

Mr. Considine was talking of the bazaars of Ispahan, and some old tiles he had bought. The one he cherished most, he said, had a design of a prince in a turban of pale petunia riding on a piebald horse, and the glaze on it was of the texture of flower-petals.

At last they came to the tea-table, leaving their bazaars and roses. The prince in the turban of pale petunia rode away on his piebald horse through the gates of the secret world.

Aunt Athene poured out the tea in that special way of hers that made everything she touched seem fragile and priceless.

'The Dean's wife has cups that are blue inside, and that always makes the tea seem a queer colour and tasteless,' she said, irrelevantly. 'And, do you know, she has redecorated their bedroom a *newly-married* pink—so trying! With blue curtains, that sentimental blue! I didn't know what to say. One feels so sorry for the Dean, who after all quotes Sir Thomas Browne in his sermons.'

'Poor fellow, poor fellow! *He* can hardly with any delight raise up the ghost of a rose,' said Mr. Considine. 'But, then, what *should* a Dean be doing in the bed of Cleopatra?'

'Hush!' said Aunt Athene, laughing. 'Are the pink sugar biscuits for Prissy? Look, Prissy, isn't that nice? Mr. Considine's housekeeper knows what little girls like.'

Oh, damn and blast her!

'I would rather have a cucumber sandwich,' said Prissy, primly.

They went on with their gay, incomprehensible conversation

as if she were not there. It was quite safe to steal glances at Mr. Considine, recalling the moments when he had played with Jane as a cat with a mouse, the delirious moments when he had broken short a sentence with a betraying word, all the moments of agony and bliss one had shared with the little governess. And that most wonderful moment of all, when he had at last declared his love and gathered her into his arms, and one had nearly fainted with delight.

But suddenly Mr. Considine took her by surprise. The blue eyes looked straight into her own, and he said, with an amused smile—'Prissy has been weighing me all this time in her invisible scales. And what, Prissy, if I may ask so personal a question, is your private opinion of me?'

Prissy gave a little gasp. It was a supreme moment. Something must be said . . . something original, extraordinary . . . Jane would have known. Oh, for words . . . words telling, arresting enough.

They came, quicker than thought, from she knew not where, in her clear, piping treble.

'I *think,* Mr. Considine,' she said, brightly and confidingly out of the innocence of her heart, 'that you are more knave than fool.'

There was a moment of silence so appalling that all the nerves in Prissy's body seemed to tingle agonizingly, and then she felt suddenly sick and very cold, as if a great clammy frog were squatting in her entrails.

A deeply-shocked sound came from Aunt Athene.

'I am *ashamed* of you,' she said, in a hissing whisper. 'Don't laugh at her, Alexis, please. If there is anything on earth one abominates, it is a pert, precocious child. I can only apologize for having brought her.'

Out of the abyss of her desolation, Prissy saw with amazement that Mr. Considine was convulsed with silent laughter. He was in a paroxysm of mirth that seemed to come from deep inside him, and was betrayed only by the quivering of his mouth and the twitching of his nostrils. Time stood still while he laughed and laughed, and Aunt Athene sat there looking as if a serpent had stung her.

'I don't know when I've had such a dusting,' he said, at last, drying his eyes. 'What have I done, Prissy, what have I done . . . ?'

But the pain in Prissy's throat prevented speech. The other world had crashed about her ears. She was smirched and degraded. She had humiliated Aunt Athene, and though Mr. Considine had laughed, he must, in his heart, think her a cheap and common girl. He and Aunt Athene had beautiful minds . . . Oh! you could tell they had, with their talk on music and Cleopatra and the ghost of a rose. So beautiful.

Aunt Athene turned sideways in her chair, as if she could no longer bear the sight of Prissy, and Mr. Considine began to talk hurriedly. They took no more notice of her. She was cast into outer darkness, she was with the lost and the damned.

Presently Aunt Athene rose to go, gathering up her gloves, and looking in the little glass in her handbag at her cool disdainful face.

'Wait a moment,' said Mr. Considine. 'There is something in the next room I'd like to show Prissy.'

Aunt Athene, with a faint shrug of her shoulders, sat down again.

'Come, Prissy,' said Mr. Considine, smiling down at her.

It was terribly kind; but it would only make matters worse, thought Prissy, wretchedly.

Mr. Considine shut the door of his study, and led her to a cabinet, on the shelves of which, neatly arranged and labelled, was a collection of strange and interesting objects.

'Look, Prissy, at this pink shell. If you hold it to your ear, you can hear the voice of the sea.'

He took out the great cold shell and put it into her hands. It had lovely curves, and ribbed lips, and on the delicate rose-colour were freckles of brown. The tears poured down Prissy's cheeks as she held it obediently to her ear.

'You know,' said Mr. Considine, 'I wouldn't show this collection to your aunt. She wouldn't care about it. But to me, shells are such . . . *enchanted* things. This one is for you, because you are . . . rather a fairy kind of person.'

'Me!' said Prissy, with quivering lips. She could hardly believe her ears. 'I was so awful . . . I don't know why I said it.'

She began to cry now as if her heart would break.

'My dear child, I think it is the most delightful thing that has ever been said to me,' said Mr. Considine. He put an arm about her, stooped, and kissed her cheek.

Oh, holy smoke! Oh, God!

The real world and the secret world clashed soundlessly together, like two meteors colliding in space. They fused and became one.

In a daze, she followed Aunt Athene down the stairs and out into the street. Her feet seemed scarcely to touch the earth. Aunt Athene walked on in silence, still in her punishing mood. But she couldn't reach Prissy in her secret world. She had only pity now for Aunt Athene and all other women; the shut-out, the unblessed. For was she not Jane's counterpart, her equal?

The Little Willow

THE first evening, Simon Byrne was brought to the house by a friend of Charlotte's, one of those with whom she would have to settle an account after the war—unless, of course, he didn't come back. The stranger stood on the threshold and took in the room, and a look of such extraordinary delight came over his face that the youngest Miss Avery's heart gave a little leap, almost as if, independently of her mind and will, it greeted of its own accord another of its kind.

It was, of course, a peculiarly gracious room, with its high ceiling and Adam chimney piece. The shiny white walls were painted with light and dim reflections of colours, and a thick black hearthrug smudged with curly pink roses—an incongruous Balkan peasant rug in that chaste room—somehow struck a note of innocence and gaiety, like the scherzo in a symphony. That rug, and the photographs on the lid of the grand piano; the untidy stack of books on a table; and a smoky pseudo old master over the fireplace, with the lily of the Annunciation as a highlight, a pale question mark in the gloom, gave the room an oddly dramatic quality. Lisby had often thought—'It is like a room on the stage, in which the story of three sisters is about to unfold.'

The passing reflections of Charlotte in red, Brenda in green made a faint shimmer on the walls as they drifted about, as if a herbaceous border were reflected momentarily in water.

'Charlotte dear, I've brought a friend. He was at Tobruk. Comes from South Africa, and doesn't know a soul over here,' said Stephen Elyot. 'He's just out of hospital.'

'I am so glad!' said Charlotte glowingly, giving him both her hands. 'You must come as often as you like.'

His eyes dwelt on her dark, lovely face, and he said, 'You don't know what it feels like to be in a drawing-room again.'

'I can very well imagine. It must feel like the peace of God,'

said Brenda, in that soft, plangent voice of hers, which was so
perfect an instrument for the inspired remarks that seemed to fall
effortlessly from her lips.

She could say the most divinely right things without a throb
of real sympathy, and would spend pounds on roses rather
than write a letter of condolence. As for her 'cello playing, it
was strange how deeply she could move one, while she herself
remained quite aloof. It was because she knew what the music
was meant to say and was thinking about the music all the time,
and not of how she played or how she felt. It was a great charm
in her.

Lisby said nothing. She had no poetic conception of herself to
impose on the minds of others. However, she had her uses. She
cut the sandwiches and made the coffee and threw herself into
the breach when some unassuming guest seemed in danger of
being neglected. And unassuming guests often were. Charlotte
and Brenda had such brilliant friends—musicians and artists and
writers. The truest thing about those girls was that they were
charmers. Every other fact sank into insignificance beside that
one supreme quality. Though each had her own strongly marked
individuality, they had this in common: that by lamplight they
acquired, in their trailing dresses, a timeless look, as if they might
have stood for types of the seductive woman in any age. Not a
modern girl; but the delicate creature who through the ages has
been man's rose of beauty, or his cup of hemlock.

Always, destroying friendship, there was this allure—the
glow, the fragrance, the what-you-will, which, sooner or later,
ensnared every young man and made him the captive of one or
the other of the two elder Misses Avery.

'Charlotte dear,' said Stephen Elyot, wandering about the
room with his coffee cup in his hand, 'I wonder, with your exquisite taste, you let that picture hang there! It's all *wrong,* my dear,
as I've told you before. A Watteau, now, or a Fragonard, for this
eighteenth-century room. And yet your *décors* for the stage are so
perfect! You are *quite* my favourite designer.'

'Lisby would die if we banished the picture. It's been in the
family for generations,' said Charlotte.

'It has been loved by people who are dead, for its . . . holiness, not for aesthetic reasons; and that makes it spiritually precious,' Simon Byrne said in a low voice to Lisby, by whom he chanced to be sitting.

She gave a little start. The thick white paint of the lily, and its golden tongue, had fascinated her as a child, making all lilies seem not quite earthly flowers. How did he know so quickly that the dark picture in the white room brought spiritual values into it, brought her mother saying, 'Yes, darling; perhaps the angel has a queer face—perhaps he *is* a little bit like Miss Nettleton. How interesting that someone we know should have a face that an old master chose for the Angel Gabriel! I shall always think of Miss Nettleton as a very special kind of person.'

'It almost seems as if he might be my kind of person,' she thought. Perhaps one would have thought his face unremarkable if one had not caught that look on it. 'He has known horror and violence, and is terribly vulnerable to beauty,' she had said to herself, with one of her flashes of insight.

Brenda played that evening, and Simon Byrne never took his eyes off her. In her long green dress, with her gold hair like an inverted sheaf of corn, she held him spellbound. Or perhaps it was the music.

When she went to bed that night, Lisby caught herself hoping quite desperately that it was, after all, the music; and for such a foolish reason. Because as he was leaving he took her little willow tree in his long thin hands.

'So cool,' he said, 'and watery. Willows and water—I used to dream of them.'

'In the desert?' she asked.

'When I was lost,' he said, 'and parched with thirst, and terribly frightened.'

'It's the loveliest thing I have,' she said.

It was made of jade and crystal and it stood on the lacquer cabinet in the hall. She had fallen in love with it in an antique shop and had expended on it, with wild extravagance, her first term's salary as a teacher. Charlotte and Brenda had thought her too utterly feckless—almost wicked. The sun by day and the moon by night made it throw a lovely shadow on the wall. She couldn't explain that what she loved was the *idea* of a willow that had been in the mind of the Chinese artist—the glitter and coolness and bewitchment. But he would know.

He came several times. 'Naturally,' thought Lisby, 'one would like the house, wouldn't one? Its oldness and peace.' And Charlotte arranged the flowers so beautifully and there were music and conversation: Brenda and her friends practising their quartets for concerts and Charlotte's friends talking of art. Anyone could come to the Court House as a place in which to forget the war. There was the strangeness of its being so near London and yet completely hidden in a wood, an oasis in the desert of ribbon development that had spread around it in the past few years. Many young men on leave found it a place of refuge.

He was a person one could talk to. The things that made Lisby laugh made him laugh too. Sometimes he would catch her eye and they would go off into a silent fit of laughter at some absurd thing that no one else had remarked. She knew, once or twice, the strange feeling of strings being plucked in her mind by a chance word or gesture of his, and he had a way of humming some tune that had been haunting her, even something she had not heard for a long time: a phrase from a symphony, perhaps, that had suddenly come back to her quite distinctly between sleeping and waking, as if a record had been put on in her mind.

And then, one day, Brenda, in her delicate way, appropriated his friendship. A person versed in Brenda-ish modes of behaviour could guess what she thought. When she said charming things a little frostily, as if offering an ice-chilled gardenia, when she smiled with dazzling sweetness one moment and raised her eyebrows rather coldly the next, one knew what was in her mind. She was dealing with a situation that required delicacy and tact. Love was sacred, even unwanted love. The little flame must not be allowed to go out. So one blew on it prettily one moment, and damped it down the next. For a conflagration meant the end of everything, it meant stamping on the heart in which it burned. And how, in wartime, could one bear to do that?

She said, 'You know, Simon is rather an intriguing person. He can say rather divine things—when one is alone with him. Still waters, my dear, run deep.'

Yes. He wouldn't wear his heart on his sleeve. But to be the person to whom he said 'rather divine things' must be to feel oneself unimaginably exquisite.

There was that night they all went out into the garden when the all clear sounded. The scent of the tobacco plants was so sweet it was like a presence, like a naked nymph following one about, and the moon was so bright that the red roses kept their colour, and the white were luminous like the moths. Standing apart, Lisby was fascinated by his shadow lying clear-cut on the lawn. She stared at it, and then, looking up, saw it printed, gigantic, across the sky. It gave her a queer cold feeling, seeming to confirm an idea she had had of him lately: that everything he was concerned in here and now was the beginning of something that would go on happening outside this sphere. It would always be there, behind her eyelids.

After that, she couldn't go on trying to make up to him for the times that Brenda was too much occupied with someone else to bother about him. It would be a kind of mockery. The only thing was to keep out of his way.

But the last evening of his embarkation leave, when he came to say good-bye, it was she who had to see him to the front door. Brenda was fey that night, with a kind of febrile gaiety, because the favoured lover of the moment was home on forty-eight hours' leave, and she had no eyes for anyone but him; and Charlotte was deeply involved with Richard Harkness. When they said good-bye, they would doubtless be driven into each other's arms. One could see it in their eyes when they looked at each other.

Lisby's eyes fell on the little willow. She seized it and put it into his outstretched hand. 'Please take it—for luck,' she said.

'But you can't give this away, Miss Avery. It's—it's ... much too lovely,' he stammered.

'Please, please—it's more yours than mine.'

'It's terribly kind of you. Your sisters—you've been so kind letting me come. I shall dream of this house.'

'But you'll come again,' said Lisby, speaking as lightly as she could.

'I'd try to ... in the spirit, if not in the flesh,' he said, with his crooked smile. Why must he say a thing so devastating?

'Look at Orion—like some secret heavenly diagram,' said Lisby at the open door, because she had no word of comfort for him. (Oh, dear! He'll think I'm trying to be appealing, trying to be a poetical little puss, trying to get at him, she thought despairingly.) If only Brenda would come out for a moment and be very sweet in that way she had of being responsive to another's mood! She could have given him something to take away with him, some cryptic remark, that he could dwell upon and cherish, as if it were a tiny key she had put into his hand to unlock a door in the future. But she was caught away into a private heaven, and so he had to go without any hope.

He looked up at the heartbreaking glitter of Orion, so serene, so triumphant above the tortured world. 'A lover might use it as a code,' he said, almost under his breath. 'Abelard signing his letters to Heloise.'

He looked down at her, hesitating a moment, as if there were something he wanted to say. And then, with a sigh, he turned away. As he looked back at the gate to salute her, the little tree in his hand caught the starlight and shone with a faint blue fire.

He never wrote. Lisby, sorting out the post, sometimes looked wonderingly at a letter addressed to Brenda in a hand-writing she didn't know, but the name on the flap of the envelope was never his.

When the war was over at last, Richard Harkness, liberated from a prison camp in Germany, came back to claim Charlotte. Their wedding was fixed for the autumn.

'By the way, Brenda,' Charlotte said casually one day, looking up from a letter she was writing, 'I forgot to tell you. Richard says that Simon Byrne was a prisoner in the same Offlag. He died last year.'

'Oh, poor darling!' said Brenda, in the sweet, hollow voice she used when the conventions demanded an assumption of sorrow. One's heart had been wrung so often that there had come a time when it recorded merely a mechanical spasm. She went on arranging the flowers with a set expression.

Lisby said nothing. She sat very still in the recesses of the armchair and clasped her knees to still their trembling. 'So much death, one cannot bear it,' she said at last, and got herself out of the room somehow. She always took things to heart—as if she suffered in her own body the agony of unknown millions.

'It's all very well for Lisby,' said Brenda with a shrug. 'But, after all, she hasn't had any *personal* loss in this war. Not like you and me. I mean, when someone's killed who's been in love with one, it makes it all so terribly poignant. I sometimes think I've felt so much, I can't feel any more. Those poor lambs!' She sighed and dipped her face into the roses, as if she would leave with them the expression of grief she could now decently abandon. It was almost as though she were leaving them on his grave to symbolise her thoughts of him, that would fade more quickly than they. 'He was sweet, but rather dumb,' she said.

'Did he ever——' asked Charlotte, looking over her tortoise-shell glasses.

'Not in so many words. You all took it for granted it was me. But perhaps, after all, *you* were the attraction, Charlotte.' But the hint of doubt found no expression in the tones of her voice.

'Or Lisby. It really is rather awful the way we leave her out of account.'

Charlotte sealed her letter and took off her glasses. She had a face like La Belle Ferronière, on which the glasses had the air of an amusing affectation. But Brenda had the flowerlike delicacy of a Piero della Francesca. Lisby had seen the resemblances and had made her sisters a present of them. But no one had noticed that she herself was like the watching girl who holds a basket on her head in the background of El Greco's *Christ in the Temple.*

'Of course,' said Charlotte, affixing a stamp, 'it wasn't I. That's a thing I never make a mistake about. A woman always knows.'

'Well, I am not so cocksure about love as you seem to be. I mean, I'm inclined to say to myself, '*If* he does so and so, *if* he remembers what hat I wore the day before yesterday, *if* he bothers to look up the address I'm staying at in the telephone book, *then* I shall know for certain. But I don't remember applying any such tests to Simon. Somehow we never got that far. Though I had my suspicions, of course.'

Brenda carried the roses across the room and put them on

the piano, in the midst of the numerous photographs, of young men in uniform. Surreptitiously she changed the place of one. He had been shot down over Hamburg, and his place was among the dead. Perhaps no one but herself, who was responsible for it, was aware of this arrangement of the photographs. She had a feeling about the matter of which she would not have spoken for the world. It did not exactly amount to a superstition. Perhaps it meant no more than did the meticulous dividing up of her books into their respective categories. It irritated her to find a novel thrust in between two volumes of poetry. Death, perhaps, was poetry, and life, prose. Or was it the other way round?

In the midst of preparations for the wedding, no one, it seemed, gave another thought to Simon Byrne.

'Lisby seems rather odd these days—sort of strung-up,' said Charlotte one day. 'Do you think, Brenda, that subconsciously she minds my getting married and your being engaged? I mean, it can't be much fun, poor child, seeing happiness through other people's eyes, as Shakespeare has already remarked.' She snapped off a thread and took the pins out of a seam.

Brenda looked down with a preoccupied expression at the ring on her long pale hand, where it lay on a fold of crêpe de Chine she had been sewing. 'How incredibly lucky we are that our two have come through alive!' she said. 'Gerald doesn't know *how* lucky he is; because it *might* have been John. I don't know, but I *think* it might have been. I was devastated when he was killed. I dare say you are right about Lisby. But what can we do . . . ?'

'That cyclamen colour you've chosen for the bridesmaids—of course, you'll look divine in it, but it's trying for Lisby. Heaven knows, she's sallow enough.'

'But, my dear, what was I to do? We had the stuff and we've got no coupons. If only Gerald were back, we could have had a double wedding and both got out of Lisby's way. I feel we rather swamp her, you know—like two arc lamps putting out the moonlight. Now, isn't that a tribute to our Lis?'

Charlotte was married on a golden day. While they waited for her in the porch, Lisby thought that Brenda looked more like an Italian primitive than ever, pale and bright as an angel. (But we are all wrong for the blue horizon and the golden leaves—too shrill, too springlike, she thought.) Their reflections stained with pink the dew-drops in a spider's web slung between two tombstones.

A cab drove up to the lich gate, and Charlotte came down the path on the arm of an uncle, her dark eyes shining through her veil. She was so majestic, so withdrawn that they did not venture to speak to her, but spread out her train, whispering nervously together.

Richard Harkness stood at the altar steps. To Lisby he had rather a vulpine look. It argued a certain spirituality in Charlotte, not to be deceived by outward appearances, but to swoop unerringly on the qualities she wanted. But he hadn't been Simon's sort. He had never mentioned Simon's name in Lisby's presence. She was grateful to him for that, but she couldn't forgive him.

She stole a glance apprehensively at the best man. He had been in the camp too—a doctor, they said. He had a dark, ascetic face, sensitive and melancholy. One must keep out of his way.

The wedding reception was like any other: the strained hilarity, the desperate frivolity, lit with a perilous brightness as of unshed tears. Corks popped, the cake was cut, the toasts proposed. Charlotte came out of her trance, and Richard made a speech so charming that all her friends began to think they knew, after all, what she saw in him.

There was Brenda by the window, trying desperately to make conversation with Captain Oliver. When her voice was high and strained like that, one knew she was wilting, and there were those faint mauve shadows under her eyes. The man was difficult. He appeared to have no capacity for small talk.

'By the way, did you come across someone who was a friend of mine—Simon Byrne? He was in the tanks,' she said.

Brenda ... don't ... Don't! Lisby cried out soundlessly, with a pain like cramp about her heart. His name seemed to sound through the room like a clash of cymbals. She felt that it must pierce every breastbone. It made a stranger of Brenda. It was incomprehensible that she could use it to make conversation, that to her it could be a name like any other.

Lisby saw the start that Captain Oliver gave. He turned quickly and looked at Brenda—a long, searching look.

'Yes, I knew Byrne,' he said.

'He was such a dear. We liked him so much. Look, Charlotte has gone up to change. I must fly after her.'

They were gone at last. Charlotte leaned out and waved. Someone threw a slipper after the taxicab.

In the throng at the gate, Lisby was aware of Captain Oliver edging his way toward her.

'Miss Avery,' he said in her ear, 'may I speak to you a moment alone?'

'In the morning room,' said Lisby, very pale. For some unfathomable reason she picked up her bouquet from the hall table before preceding him into the little yellow room.

A picture glowing with evening appeared in the frame of the window. In the foreground, the black trunk of the mulberry tree, about which still dangled a few heart-shaped leaves of sour green, and to the right the long silver plumes of the pampas grass, had a strange significance, as if the words 'black, gold, silver' were being reiterated in a poem. The blue October mist lay beyond, veiling the lawn, and a little sumac tree burned like a torch at the edge of the mist. A bird that had abandoned music for the winter made a grasshopper sound.

The pampas grass. Charlotte had tried to dig it up—a vulgar interloper, she had said. Lisby clung desperately to her thoughts. She did not want to hear what this man had to say. She sank down on the sofa and began mechanically to take her bouquet to pieces. The colour was drained out of her face, and she looked ghastly in the cyclamen shade that was so becoming to Brenda.

'So you knew Simon Byrne,' said Captain Oliver, looking down at her. 'I wonder ... perhaps you could help me, Miss Avery? I was with him when he died.'

'Have you, perhaps, a message ... for my sister?' asked Lisby faintly, arranging little sprigs of heather on her knee.

'That's what I don't know,' he said with a sigh. 'There is something I'd like to tell someone—but not the wrong person. You see, Simon meant a great deal to me. Could you tell me, did she ever give him a little tree, a willow? I suppose it was one of those Chinese things.'

'No,' said Lisby, very low, 'she never gave him anything.'

'I am going to tell *you*,' said Captain Oliver, as if making a sudden decision. 'A secret would be safe with you, wouldn't it? He was badly hurt, you know. His wound never healed. He was terribly ill all the time; but the odd thing was that through it all, he was never less than himself. They couldn't do anything to Simon. They couldn't strip him of a single one of his qualities. It was as if he had some inward source of happiness, a core of peace in his heart. The camp was short of doctors and they were only too pleased to make use of me, so I was able to make things a little easier for him.'

'I am glad,' she said, bent over her flowers, 'that he had you to look after him.'

'The night before he died,' went on Captain Oliver, in a low deliberate voice, 'he dictated a letter to his mother in South Africa. He was a bit of a poet, you know. It was a very touching letter. I suppose she has it now, poor soul. I said, "Is there no one else, Simon?" He shook his head. "There was a girl," he said, "but she never knew she was my girl." I asked him to tell me about her, thinking it might comfort him. He said, "She is a little, quiet creature—like mignonette—and her eyes go light and dark with her thoughts. I knew in my bones she was meant for me. Once, when the pain was very bad, I thought she came and kissed me. I felt her cheek against mine. It was soft and cool—like young buds, as I always imagined it would be. And the pain went away and I went to sleep. You know, Robert, she wouldn't mind my dreaming that. She has such exquisite compassion. When I said good-bye, she gave me the loveliest thing she had—a little willow tree. It was smashed to bits in my kit when the shell got us." I thought to myself, "Perhaps she did care, that girl." He died toward morning, very peacefully, without speaking again.'

Lisby sat very still. 'So cold . . . so cold,' she said, chafing her hands as if the hands of the dying lay between them.

'So *you* were his girl,' said Robert Oliver.

'He was my dear, dear love,' whispered Lisby. She bowed her head on her knees and wept soundlessly.

He thought, 'It is sad for a girl when her first avowal of love has to be made to a third person'. And, going softly to the door, he turned the key in the lock and let himself out by the window.

'Lisby cried her eyes out after you left,' wrote Brenda to Charlotte. 'But at night she looked so radiant, one might have thought it was *her* wedding day. There were dozens of letters for you by the evening post (I've sent them on) and some for me. I sorted them out, and said, as one usually does, "None for you, I'm afraid, Lisby darling." She looked at me so strangely, and said; "I have had mine—one that was never written." What could she have meant? I said, "What on earth do you mean?" But I knew from the look on her face that it is one of those things she will never tell.'

Don Juan and the Lily

I WAS brought up a child of light. There were no dark corners in our house, and none, it was assumed, in our minds, which, said my mother, were an open book to her. She was so ingenuous herself that she did not conceal from us her true opinion of our characters and our looks, and early discouraged us, for our own good, from entertaining what she called silly ideas. It seemed—look at Aunt May and Aunt Nora!—that the women of the Craigie family never married, and we were true Craigies. And yet in *her* family all five sisters became engaged on leaving the schoolroom. What it was that the Hardwicks had and the Craigies hadn't she didn't tell us. These things are a mystery. But we were not to mind. Some of the very nicest women she knew were old maids, and she wasn't at all sure that they hadn't, after all, had the best of it.

My father put down the newspaper and looked thoughtfully out of the window. I don't know what he saw with his mind's eye, but it may have been something rather sad. Perhaps he felt a little like the Forsaken Merman, only the other way round—a mortal who had married a mermaid called back to her cold sea-world.

She was so cool and crisp, she seemed to lower the temperature when she entered a room. With her bustling air of always having to do everything that had to be done in our house—our efforts and the maids' met with little appreciation—she seemed to be rushing on a surging wave up and down the stairs, through the rooms and the corridor. When one was feverish, her firm white hands, cold as alabaster, had a kind of salty healing in their touch.

Perhaps it was the lightness and airiness of our lives and the assumption that we could have no secrets that made me hanker a little after darkness and mystery, that made me prefer *Wuthering Heights* (and even *St. Elmo*) to Jane Austen, Westminster Abbey to St. Paul's and Miss Georgia Dellow to the other employees of the great industrial concern that opened its portals to me at the age of nineteen, an unwilling victim of my mother's belief that her daughters' lack of allure necessitated their having careers—modest ones, since, so far as she could see, none of them showed any talent for anything in particular.

The Company was housed in a great sham-Gothic, dusty building in the heart of the City, which, if mere darkness had been enough, should have pleased me. But the shadows cast by romance are stained with Tyrian dyes, and this was an oppressive twilight, alleviated above each desk by a green moon of porcelain over a naked electric bulb. The lack of light and air fretted the nerves, and what air there was seemed vitiated by the smell of copying-ink and gum, and, mingled with it, a strange too-heavy funereal scent.

'You will sort this and file that and write these names in the card index,' said Miss Grouse, whose name matched her person. She looked at me as if I were a new sort of grub.

'What!' I said. 'All day long? Don't I do anything with my brains?'

There was a horrid silence while a dozen heads looked up from the miscellaneous litter on a dozen squares of pink blotting-paper, and the stare of a dozen pairs of inimical eyes intimated that I was indeed a grub and a very queer one.

'Well, I never!' said a voice, and then someone laughed, a cool, gurgling laugh like a bubble of water. I looked towards the sound in a hunted way, and met a gaze that was not unfriendly.

'Poor little thing! She doesn't know yet that brains are a disadvantage, not to speak of heart and imagination,' said the one who had laughed. I saw that there was a Madonna lily on her desk.

'Now, Miss Dellow! Disloyalty is something I will not tolerate,' said Miss Grouse, with a snap of her thin lips.

Miss Dellow did not reply, but a smile lurked behind her mysterious expression like the one on the face of the Mona Lisa. She lowered her heavy eyelids and went on manipulating with extraordinary rapidity the squares of pasteboard on her desk. She had a look as if she knew things that made it not worth while to reply . . . strange things.

She was about thirty-five and by no means pretty, the upper part of her face being too wide for the narrow jaw and little tapering chin. But her ivory skin, black hair parted in the middle, and long dark eyes gave her an attractive foreign look. She was wearing, on that occasion, a white blouse with thin black stripes and a large cameo brooch. Evidently she was addicted to cameos, for there was another in a ring on her middle finger, an enormous ring that gave her long, pale hand an important, medieval look. Suddenly I was aware of a heart of darkness, another kind of darkness altogether, in the greyish no-light. And the lily shone like one wax candle illuminating a secret shrine, a symbol and a portent. Its physical reality might be distasteful, spilling a sickly aroma into the already weighted air; but its symbolic quality brought poetry into those arid purlieus of commerce that had threatened to wither me into inanition.

That first day Miss Dellow did not speak to me, nor for several days afterwards. Every morning she came in carrying her lily in a tall glass vase, holding it reverentially before her, eyelids cast down. No one smiled at her ceremonial progress through the room, moving all of a piece, with a soft frou-frou of taffeta. Until the clock struck nine, which was the signal for work, she occupied herself with private matters, head bent over opened desk, hands moving over the miscellaneous objects collected there.

When I was at length privileged to look into Miss Dellow's desk, it was, I found, as exciting as a stall in some Oriental bazaar, and as neat as a paper of bright new pins. After the brief flowering time of lilies, when there was none to overpower the fainter scents of less ecclesiastical flowers, a delicious whiff of attar of roses emanated from the silver foil lining of the desk, on which she had sprinkled a few drops from a tiny flask from Persia. A garish box of Turkish Delight, a packet of very special tea (office tea tasting, she said, like hay—with a dash of manure, she added sardonically), sticks of delicately coloured sealing-wax, an old seal, lavender-tinted writing-paper headed with a silver G entwined in a love-knot, an *edition de luxe* of the *Rubaiyat of Omar Khayyam,* packets of letters tied up with blue ribbon ('I have to keep my letters here, having a rather nosey Mamma,' she explained, with a droop of her eyelids) were among the treasures over which she hovered each morning, afterwards locking her desk and slipping the key into her handbag.

But I am anticipating. A very disagreeable incident was the cause of Miss Dellow's first speaking to me. One day, a man I had never seen before came into the office. He was a pallid, thin man, with a wave of brown hair over a high forehead, and a slight limp, and he looked, I thought, different from the other officials who sometimes sauntered into our department, usually to complain of our deficiencies ... as if he might think other things more important than work, as if he might even take a day off in the spring to go and hear the cuckoo.

But my first pleasant impression was quickly effaced. He went up to Miss Grouse's desk, and after some conversation between them, I heard my name called.

'Miss Craigie, are these your initials?'

'Why, yes,' I said, confronted with a pencilled 'E.L.C.' on a document.

Miss Grouse looked down her nose, with a pained expression.

'She is new, Mr. Pelham. I am sorry. Her work should have been checked.'

'Young lady,' said this Mr. Pelham, swinging round and regarding me with a kind of pale glare like our cat Lucifer's, 'you have given me a considerable amount of trouble. You have, indeed, caused the waste of a whole morning's work.' He spread out his fingers with the gesture of someone throwing away the fragments of a torn-up letter, as if consigning his wasted moments to limbo.

'Good gracious!' I said, surprised to discover that anything I did amiss in the course of my meaningless duties could set up repercussions of any kind.

'In a most ... *lighthearted* manner, you,' said Mr. Pelham, 'have ... *secreted*' (again that curious pause and emphasis, as if the *mot juste* were being sought in his mind and run to earth) 'an important document in the wrong file; and until you have learnt that there is, after all, some reason, if not rhyme, in our methods, you had better confine your activities to ... to ... licking stamps, and so forth. Will you see to that, Miss Grouse?'

And he limped out, without a glance to left or right.

'Beast!' I muttered. 'Cruel, official beast!' and went back to my place with scorched cheeks and tears of mortification in my eyes. I almost began to credit Lucifer, our cat, with transmigratory powers, and certainly to ascribe some of his qualities to this anti-pathetic person. Lucifer's way with young thrushes, shrewmice, and even butterflies, had not endeared him to me. And I had never liked his expression.

'Insulting!' said the girl next me. 'But he's like that. Very superior and sarcastic. I wouldn't be in Dellow's shoes . . . though she gets on with him all right. She'd get on with the Devil,' she added, darkly.

So it was this man whose bell Miss Dellow had to answer. But I had noticed that whereas the other senior clerks seized their notebooks and ran to answer the summons of their chiefs, she drifted out in a leisurely way and, when she returned, always sat and worshipped her lily a moment before going to the typing room.

'He won't have anyone but Dellow. She's terribly good, you know—by far the best worker we've got.'

Presently, I found her at my elbow, the desks on either side of me being for the moment vacant. She turned over some of my papers, ostensibly looking for something, and with a sideways glance in my direction she said—'So you've been on the carpet! Don't take it too much to heart, child. He shouldn't be in an office, really; it gets him down. I'll tell you something. He writes poetry in his spare time, and the two don't go together. But don't pass that on . . . they wouldn't understand.' She was stacking up my letters into several neat piles as she talked, creating an illusion of work. 'You don't like it here? Well, I could see that.'

'Oh, I want . . . I want . . . to do nothing at all, just to be happy,' I said, despairingly; 'or else to do something that really matters. I *can't* stay here all my life.'

'You won't have to, mark my words,' she said, with her mys-terious smile. 'One day I'll be dressing a doll for a baby-girl with a mouth like her mother's. You have a very sweet mouth, you know. And lovely hair. Someone's going to fall for you before very long.'

And with these strange consoling words (and yet too sugared, too cloying to the taste, inducing a faint feeling of nausea), she glided away, forestalling the admonition that was about to fall from the lips of Miss Grouse, who had transfixed us with a stare.

After this our intimacy grew apace, though I couldn't imagine Miss Dellow in any other surroundings. Her private life was a closed book to me. I could not visualize her in my own milieu and dismissed the idea of inviting her for a week-end so soon as it came into my head. What would happen to that heart of darkness in the clarity of our atmosphere?

There are people who are enclosed in their own personality as in a globe, of something less substantial than air, impalpable, invisible, and yet felt with the sixth sense that apprehends the imponderable, and seen with the eye of the mind that perceives the irradiation of some ghostly spectrum. I knew, in some obscure way, that Georgia's mystery would dissolve in our lightness and brightness. My mother's blue eyes, her breezy laughter, would destroy it. And a Georgia without her aura would be like a saint bereft of his mandola.

I never got to the point of asking her about her lily, Miss Brice, the shrewd little Cockney who sat next to me, having once let fall a comment that sealed my lips.

'Dellow and her suffocating lily!' she said. 'One of her gentlemen friends told her—Pelham, most likely; it seems he tells her some very queer things—that she's the living image of an Italian Madonna, and she's terribly taken with the idea.'

Lucifer, I thought sadly, would be the only member of our household with whom Georgia would feel at home.

But I couldn't believe she confided any secrets about Mr. Pelham to the others. Only to me, I believed, did she ever open her lips about that egregious person. I had seen no more of him. The impact of his personality was felt only in the sharp ping of the bell that summoned Miss Dellow, and in the fact that she always returned with a dim smile sunk, as it were, below the surface of her face and but faintly shining through.

'He's in one of his moods this afternoon,' she'd say to me. 'I think he only rang because he needed a little soothing. I don't know what it is about me—it's a gift, I suppose, and I don't take any credit for it—but I do seem to be a solace to people. You know, they' (she slid her eyes over the rows of bent heads) 'are all frightened of him; he doesn't suffer fools gladly, of course. But he'd eat out of my hands.'

I looked down at those shapely members gliding about like fishes in the pool of her desk, touching this and that, and a vision of my enemy stooping his lips to take lumps of Turkish Delight from those curled fingers came into focus before my eyes. 'I'm supposed to have healing hands,' she went on, and another vision slipped into the place of the first, of fingers stroking a pallid brow, sweeping back a wave of brown hair.

And once, returning from one of her mysterious interviews, she said—'If you've once seen a man cry, you can't but have quite a different feeling about him, a *tendresse*.'

'Cry?' I said. My heart felt suddenly hollow and chill, like an old nest into which some cold drops of rain had fallen. For some reason the blood rushed to my head, and even my ears tingled.

'You see, Elsa,' she whispered, behind the raised lid of her desk, 'sometimes men want something you can't give them. Not a fastidious creature like me. Pure as a lily and brave as a lion— that's my ideal. You have to live up to your ideals, don't you? You'll think it peculiar, my talking to you like this; but you and I are the only people here of what I call heart and imagination . . . except him, of course.'

I felt sick with shame to know things of my enemy that gave me an unfair advantage over him. Or—was it possible?—gave him an unfair advantage over me.

It was soon after this that Georgia invited me for the first time to visit her home. I was full of curiosity, but reluctant to go. It is one thing to watch enraptured an angel-fish going through its convolutions behind plate glass, and quite another to be asked to enter its tank. Miss Dellow's home, I felt, would be an extension of the narrow sphere that contained her in the office, and I was doubtful of being able to breathe its air.

'Pure as a lily and brave as a lion,'—I remembered, following her down into the Tube. An invisible banner seemed to float over her, bearing this proud device. I almost expected the other passengers to be aware of it, to look at her with interest and wonder. But their faces were as blank, their eyes as lustreless as usual, their thoughts flown back to the business they had left, or forward to whatever awaited them at the end of the journey. Dull thoughts, thought I with youthful bitterness, little wriggling thoughts like earwigs. I condemned them all, men hidden behind newspapers, or staring vacantly into space, women fiddling in their handbags. No one was thinking about beauty.

I turned to look at Miss Dellow. She, too, was fiddling in her bag, and looked, after all, in her hat and coat, like anyone else, as if the dry air and the smell of warm rubber had withered the romance in her.

She took me to a tall Victorian house in a Bayswater terrace and opened the door with a latch-key.

'Do the two of you live here all alone?' I asked.

'Not at all. I have let off the top floors and the basement. You'd be surprised what a good business woman I am, Elsa.'

'No, I am not surprised. I should think you'd be good at anything.'

'Well, apart from writing novels and playing the piano, I can do most things,' she said, complacently, 'and I think I could do those, if I put my mind to it.'

She opened a door and ushered me into a room with a patterned wallpaper of blue-birds and roses and great shabby leather chairs. I knew a moment of dismay. The windows were closed, there were no flowers, no books, and nothing on the chimney-piece but an 'art' photograph of Georgia, in profile, with a veil over her head, looking raptly at—what, but a Madonna lily? A spiritless gas-fire hissed in the fireplace.

A large, rather untidy, woman, got up out of a chair. She had a swarthy, heavy face and warm dark eyes.

'This is Miss Elsa Craigie, mother.'

'Pleased to meet you, dear,' said Mrs. Dellow.

'If you'll excuse me, I'll get the tea. Now, don't be too chatty, mother,' said Georgia. 'Don't go giving away all my secrets that you think you know,' with a heavy-lidded smile at me to indicate that this was mere badinage.

'She hasn't any,' Mrs. Dellow confided to me when the door closed on her daughter. 'Annie was always one for making a mystery out of nothing.'

'Annie? I thought . . . Georgia,' I said, faintly.

'Annie she was christened, and Annie she will always be; whatever fancy names she likes her friends to call her.'

'Come and take off your things while the kettle boils,' said Georgia, opening the door unexpectedly.

'I couldn't get in to tidy your room, Annie. You'd locked the door and taken the key.'

'You know I always do my room before I go,' said Georgia, impatiently.

'All that junk! You can't have time.'

Georgia's room would be different, I thought. All the beautiful things would be collected there, what Mrs. Dellow called 'junk'.

But 'junk', after all, was the right word. Junk, I thought, from a dismantled old provincial theatre, vermilion upholstery, gilt cherubs and all. And, like actors who had just taken part in some lurid melodrama, a troupe of dolls sprawled on a day-bed . . . limp, long-legged, fantastic dolls with decadent faces, gipsy, Pompadour, pierrot, ballerina. How could Georgia bear to share the night-hours with those wicked puppets?

But my growing horror found its culmination in the pictures that hung on the walls. Goodness knows where she had collected them. They seemed to be illustrations of the story of Don Juan Tenorio (probably cuttings from some Early Victorian chapbook) and were so crudely tinted that the violent colours ran into each other. That Georgia should choose to surround herself with scenes of seduction was strange enough, but that she should tolerate the tawdriness and vulgarity of these abominable prints seemed to reveal something so meretricious in her soul that I suddenly found myself longing never to have to see her again.

'My children, the only ones I care to have,' said Georgia, pointing to the dolls . . . evoking a phantom lily. (I could almost smell once more the heavy funereal scent). She picked up a doll and turned up its skirts. 'See how beautifully she is dressed, down to the minutest detail. She even has a brassière,' she said. But she did not mention the pictures.

When I left the house that evening, the November air seemed very cold and clean.

But I couldn't easily shake off Georgia's influence. She dominated my thoughts, sharing them with another figure, one whom she herself had called into being. She had made a legend out of the invisible Mr. Pelham, and legends have a way of taking on a life of their own. They betake themselves to the strange underworld below the upper levels of consciousness and there cut nightmarish capers. I couldn't get Don Juan out of my head.

When Georgia took her holiday the following spring, the office seemed a different place. It was as if an exuberant fountain that had kept damp a lush, romantic grotto in the depths of my being had been cut off.

Mr. Pelham, I supposed, was also away. But one afternoon his bell rang. Miss Grouse's eye, looking wildly round an almost empty room—most of the staff being dispersed on various tasks about the building—fell on me.

'Mr. Pelham's bell. Will you answer it, Miss Craigie.'

I had learnt by this time not to dispute an order, so I rose, with a sinking heart. Outside, I had to ask my way of persons encountered in the passages, and at length found myself outside a door lettered in black over frosted glass—'Mr. R. W. Pelham.'

I opened the door in a state of nervous tension, strung up to face I knew not what ordeal. And suddenly something in my mind seemed to go off with a bang, like a popped paper bag. Quite a small, merry-looking man confronted me, someone who wouldn't have hurt a fly. Lucifer's *alter ego*, Georgia's sinister lover, vanished into the pale spring sunlight, delicate as primroses, that fell on a plane tree outside the tall window.

'Hello!' said the person who had taken their place. 'Oh! of course. My typist is away, I believe. I haven't seen you before, have I?'

'Yes. I'm afraid I'm not very good,' I said. 'You said I was only fit for licking stamps.'

'Good Lord! what a brute! It must have been a day when all this tomfoolery,' waving his hand at the rows of ledgers, 'had got on my nerves. But, surely, I must have said "sticking", not "licking", I couldn't have said "licking", you know. I would never knowingly hurt anyone's pride. I shan't be able to forgive myself; but you must forgive me. Will you? By the way, are you fond of music?'

'I could listen to Chopin all night and all day,' I said.

'Oh, Chopin! Yes, when you yearn to give a ring to someone. I never have, as yet. I mean Bach,' he said, 'and Beethoven, the one so serene that he questions nothing but asserts divine truth with perfect confidence, the other always knocking on the gates of Heaven. Or Mozart. What's he like? Like the conversation of tea-roses, do you think, or the bees in the lime-blossom?'

'I think he sounds like witty people in the Eighteenth Century saying lovely things in a formal garden,' I said, not knowing that such a thought was in my mind.

'Hooray!' said Mr. Pelham. 'You shall certainly have this ticket I've got for a concert of chamber music tonight at St. Stephen's Walbrook. I'm playing the flute.'

'I thought ... I mean, I didn't know you played anything. I thought you wrote poetry.'

'Not a line—except Latin verse at school. Not even in my undergraduate days. Polyhymnia was always my Muse. And then the War came. I read poetry in the trenches.' (He was refer-ring to the first World War, of course. The events I am narrating happened in the strange pause between the catastrophes). 'But where on earth ... ? Oh! my typist, I suppose. I have an idea that I ought to be alarmed at Miss Dellow's inventive powers. She's rather a joke, isn't she? Well, well, to business. Take this down, will you?'

'Oh, please!' I said. 'My shorthand isn't at all good. Will you go very slow.'

'I'll go slow enough for the most beautiful copperplate long-hand,' he said, opening a drawer and looking into it.

And, still looking into the drawer, he began to dictate—

'If, peradventure, Reader, it has been thy lot to waste the golden years of thy life—thy shining youth—in the irksome con-finement of an office ...'

'Charles Lamb!' I said, laying down my pen. 'I think you are laughing at me, sir.'

'Heaven forbid!' said Mr. Pelham, gravely. 'If I had my way, you wouldn't be allowed to waste the golden years. I'd send you packing. You ought to be out in the woods picking primroses, practising your Chopin, reading Shelley ... going to balls, if you like that kind of thing. Girls do, I suppose. And don't call me "sir"; though perhaps I deserve it. Those confounded stamps!'

Georgia reacted in her own inimitable way to the news, some months later, of my engagement. With her peculiar smile, which had long lost its mystery for me, she remarked, half-closing her eyes—'Of course, he wanted the moon . . . But I am sure you will make him very happy, you sweet little thing.'

My mother, on the other hand, opened her eyes very wide. 'Well, well . . . so someone has fallen in love with my funny little Elsa! I think, darling, he must be a most unusual man.'

The Rose in the Picture

M RS. POTTER was as different as possible from Mrs. Halliday, as different as the Vicarage was from Hartwell House. The two ladies and the two houses represented the boundaries, as it were, of Ursula's young experience, they provided the chiaroscuro in her picture of life.

Hartwell House, her home, was up on the hill. It was a Palladian house, as white as the shell of a cuttlefish and with something of the portly, bow-fronted elegance of a Regency buck. The antique furniture within had not been picked up at sales, but had been bequeathed to successive generations of Hallidays, and seemed in its turn to have transmitted a kind of Chippendale grace to the small-boned, slender Halliday girls. The glazed chintz with its delicate posies, the pale carpets, were an expression of something pale and delicate in Mrs. Halliday's mind. She had an antipathy to the colour red, as to all strong, violent colours; which was natural, perhaps, in a person who never seemed to go very deep into anything.

But the Vicarage, down in the village, was red. One might have expected it to be brown inside to match its little brown mistress. But it wasn't. It was rather nice, if one liked a jumble of periods and a good taste that was the negation of 'taste'. There were no faded photographs of Rome, Switzerland, or any place whatever, and no Highland cattle, such as are usually found in country vicarages. A large coloured print of the Sistine Madonna dominated the space over the drawing-room chimney-piece, and below her a Dresden china shepherdess, all roses and forget-me-nots, had a somewhat prinking and incongruous air, flanked as she was by two chaste Chinese bowls. Warm colours glowed in the rooms, indigo and Venetian red and cinnamon; as if, unlike Mrs. Halliday, Mrs. Potter delved sometimes below the surface of life. Her figure was slight but somewhat globular, reminding one of an old castor-oil bottle, though soft and cushiony to touch.

Ursula had come into contact with her uncorseted body once, when, meeting her in the churchyard one Easter morning, she had been enfolded in her arms, with the greeting—'Christ has risen, dear Ursula!' and had recognized, with a faint shock of surprise, that a mystic looked out of Mrs. Potter's rather dense brown eyes.

She said, 'Yes, indeed, Mrs. Potter, dear! Alleluia!' For she held that to fail another person in his moment of exaltation, or to show embarrassment at the exposure of a private emotion, was to be guilty of a spiritual default. In her own family it was seldom possible to test one's behaviour by this criterion, and she felt a tenderness towards Mrs. Potter for allowing her the opportunity of rising to a spiritual occasion.

But there was another reason why Mrs. Potter and the Vicarage were naturally interesting to Ursula. One was the mother of Henry, and the other was his home. She couldn't help wondering what Henry appeared like in Mrs. Potter's eyes, whether she knew at all what went on behind that dome-like brow of his.

Ursula had known him from childhood without really knowing him at all. As a little girl she had been ignored by him at Christmas parties and had suffered in consequence from a sense of inferiority. The girls Henry danced with were a few years older than she and had something about them—she had no name for this something, but she recognized it when she saw it—that she could never hope to attain. You could tell even by the way their bows were tied that they knew how to talk to boys, and that their programme would be full in a few minutes. Their dark hair curled, their cheeks had red in them, and they had impertinent little noses—all of them, so it seemed to Ursula, looking back— and Henry's full underlip pouted over their heads as he guided them expertly, looking rather bored and disdainful, through the bouncing mob of younger children. The little boys who danced with her bumped her into other couples, trod on her toes and sometimes left her abruptly, marooned, in the middle of a dance, so that she had to run away and hide in another room till the music was over. It was on one such occasion that she saw something that shocked her very much. She was hidden in an armchair, when Henry came in with his partner, a girl called Beryl something.

He shut the door behind him, looked at Beryl with a sly, incandescent smile that for some reason frightened Ursula as she had once been frightened by someone coming in wearing a mask, and then suddenly they were locked together and kissing each other . . . gobbling, as if they were starved.

Paralysed with horror and shame, Ursula didn't know what to do. She couldn't move hand or foot to make a dart out of the room, for the one thing that must at all costs be prevented was their knowledge of her presence. That she should be a witness of their greedy and furtive act made her in some way a participant, made her feel guilty and initiated; but for them to know that a despised younger child had witnessed their abandonment would be to draw down upon her a hostility she was too young and tender to bear.

But Beryl and Henry were too absorbed in each other to be aware of the trembling little eavesdropper. They kissed long and violently, and then fell apart and burst out laughing.

'Hush!' said Beryl. 'The music's stopped. Let's go.'

He opened the door softly, looked out, and then signalled to her that the coast was clear. Surprisingly, Beryl put her tongue out at him as she passed, and he called her a rude name. So, they didn't even like each other.

If they hadn't behaved as if they were doing something wicked, perhaps she would not have been so disturbed. But they had . . . like her cousins when they looked in the Bible for something horrid, and giggled, and whispered things she couldn't hear. Ursula had looked afterwards, fearfully, for herself, but hadn't found a thing.

Ever after the incident of Henry and Beryl, Ursula felt a link between herself and him. She knew something about him that no one else knew. She didn't count Beryl, who was merely a visitor and soon went away, leaving not a trace behind. She didn't count his other dancing partners, though she did not overlook the possibility that they, too, had been initiated in the same manner. If so, they were the chosen, the participators, seeing him from one angle only. But to the little outsider, he who had been a hero, too grand for her acquaintance, became an object of compassion, a kind of moral clubfoot. Let him look over her head, let him be coldly patronizing. She wasn't cast down any more. She had seen him abandoned, greedy, without dignity. There were two Henrys, and she alone knew them both, and the second put the first one out of account. She knew him better than his mother, who thought him such a wonderful, good, clever boy, winning all those scholarships and shortly going to Oxford. 'Henry,' she had heard her say, 'has never given us a moment's anxiety.' But since she grew up Ursula had felt that the two Henrys she knew might be represented by the letters A and Z, and that all the alphabet in between was unknown to her. What words did the letters form themselves into for his mother, for his unknown friends?

Now he had made a name for himself in the scientific world. One saw his name in the papers and heard him on the wireless. On the rare occasions when he came home, one met him, of course, at tea at the Vicarage, still as high-and-mighty as when he was a sixth form boy. In the old days it had been a question of being too immature to be danced with, and now it was a question of being too mediocre to be talked to. All one was offered were conventional remarks uttered in that plummy voice that made one clear one's throat in nervous sympathy, and a pale gaze that seemed too glassy to be taking one in.

So that when Ursula painted the picture that she put all her feeling about life into, she thought, 'I do not suppose there is anyone who will care for it; but the one person I could not bear to see it is that Henry Potter.' Oh! if only a poet would come and drink up with his shining eyes the Chinese white, the shell-pink and the sea-green; the dove, the rose, and the book. And then turn to one and say . . . something so exquisite that one couldn't believe one's ears. But, of course, no poet would come to Hartwell. One would be on tenterhooks if he did; for the conversation would not be on the level to which he was accustomed. In fact, it was hardly conversation at all, to judge by the standard of the parties at the house of Charles and Mary Lamb. Of course, one didn't, oneself, ever speak of the things that really matter. One doesn't in the depths of the country, where people have known each other too long to know each other at all. Mrs. Potter in the churchyard on a dewy Easter morning, all wet moss and primroses and faint topaz light, was one thing, and Mrs. Potter in the Vicarage drawing-room peering into the silver teapot was another. No one, there, would have had the bad taste to speak of God. Like the lady at the Lambs' Thursday evening, everyone would have got uneasy at the turn the conversation had taken, and would have risen to go.

Everything, almost, was tabu: ideas, because no one had any; and poetry, because no one read it. As for painting, it was looked upon with the gravest suspicion, unless it were the work of an Old Master or of a Royal Academician. Really, one could count on the fingers of one hand the topics of what passed for conversation in the village of Hartwell. But of the spirit of delight one could only speak to that other self which hides in the depth of one's being.

It was that other self who painted the picture. It rose up and took command, and out of an arrangement of still-life ... white pottery dove, pink half-blown rose, and the poem of Keats ... it had made a pattern of curves and convolutions like an arabesque of Schumann, and the colours came burgeoning and shining, delicate as petals, from some core of quiet in its soul.

'If there is a person in all the world who appreciates my picture, then that person will be my person,' said Ursula, propping the canvas against the wall.

She dipped her brushes in turpentine, gathered up her paint-box and palette, and, hearing footsteps, pushed them under the sofa. Mrs. Halliday didn't approve of the morning-room's being messed up. But the light was good there, and if one didn't sometimes disregard the unreasonable prejudices of others, where would one be? She drew a chair before the picture as the door opened. It was too private, at present, for any eye to fall on it.

'Have you seen me keys? I could have sworn I'd left 'em on the bureau,' said Mrs. Halliday. It was a trick of hers to talk like that when she mislaid things, to beguile one into regarding this tiresome habit as a rather charming trait in her character. She had a very satisfactory face. The eye could rest on it happily, as on something of gracious curves and perfect proportions. But the last person to appreciate her own face was Mrs. Halliday. She was much too busy, pruning roses, making jam, or worrying about the chair-covers, to give a thought to the regularity of her features, which she took for granted. So her beautiful face was crowned, out-of-doors, by a shapeless straw hat, beribboned or garlanded in accordance with the whim of a provincial milliner. A cardigan and tweed skirt usually completed her attire.

'The money she wastes on jerseys and scarves would buy her something heavenly from Bond Street or Paris,' said Bette, who, disregarding the lilies of the field, took a good deal of thought for her wardrobe. Bette was as clever as paint. With a bow in her hair, of some inspired colour that no one else would have thought of, and a pink camellia at her waist, she could look as if she were exquisite not only in body but in mind.

'No, I haven't seen your keys,' said Ursula, wanting her mother to go away. She was in no mood, yet, for any company but her own.

'I have the most unhelpful children. What I have done to deserve it, I don't know,' said Mrs. Halliday, searching distractedly. 'None of you ever think of anyone but yourselves.'

It was true. They didn't. They were all shut up in their private worlds like grubs in their cocoons. In spite of her tenet that one should be all things to all men, that one should never default spiritually, Ursula recognized with dismay that she was as bad as any of them; worse, in fact. More introspective, more self-contained. Why, when she did respond, it was so that she could feel good, feel herself a giving-out, sympathetic person. Her mother had a terrible power. She had the power of making one feel guilty. One awful thing that weighed on Ursula's conscience, though often it had made her giggle, was that in their absence her parents were referred to as 'The Pigs' by their children. 'Any letter from the Pigs?' Richard would ask, or Bette, or Hilary, when they went away together on a visit. One could hardly look them in the face when they got back, so serene and unconscious, so pleased with everything.

'Well, chookies,' Mrs. Halliday would say, looking about her with fresh eyes at all the old things, 'it's nice to be home again.'

On one such occasion, Ursula, feeling the twinges of remorse, had said a true, embarrassing thing,

'Mother, you really are beautiful!'

Everyone, including Mrs. Halliday, had looked most surprised, and the children not a little uncomfortable, as though their sister had violated all the canons of good taste.

'Why, chookie, what nonsense! One is as God made one,' said Mrs. Halliday. But she took Ursula by the chin, looked into her eyes, and kissed her tenderly.

Mr. Halliday said gently, with his slow smile—'I made that discovery a long time ago, my child.'

So now Ursula, feeling guilty again, began to look for the keys. She found them on the window-sill, and a figure proceeding up the drive caught her eye.

'There's that Henry Potter. Now, what can he want at this time of day?' she said.

'Oh, thank you, darling! Now Cook can have her semolina. You had better find Bette or Hilary. You are so stiff and poky with that young man, he must think you quite dislike him.'

Oh, dear! People shouldn't swoop on a hidden thing and bring it into the light of day. It made you feel like a puppy whose buried bone is an open secret.

'You see, I don't think he finds us worth talking to,' she said in a little voice, moving away from the window. 'I suppose knowing about science makes you feel very superior to ordinary people.'

'Nonsense! Scientists fall in love, I suppose, like other men.'

'*In love?*' breathed Ursula, suddenly looking very young and apprehensive. 'Oh, Mother! One couldn't imagine such a thing,' she protested, in a soft, shocked voice.

'Well, dear, there is always the possibility; though I daresay he is already involved with some clever girl at Oxford who can meet him on his own level. Now, go and open the door to him and take him into the garden. I'm much too busy to be bothered.'

Henry on the doorstep, basket in hand, said that Mrs. Halliday had promised Mrs. Potter some plums for bottling and he had been sent to fetch them. One gathered that he suffered in the Potter household: his uniqueness was known and reverenced, but not intelligently served.

So Ursula took him into the garden, past the rose-beds, and

down the yew-walk. At the end of the path was a stone basin matted with the leaves of water-lilies; and a pink bud or two floating in between.

> My love is like a nenuphar,
>   My love is like a rose.
> Her shadow like a young gazelle
>   Before her softly goes,

said Henry. 'Excuse me, Ursula. You have such a romantic garden.'

'Not quite Christina Rossetti,' said Ursula, walking on sedately; 'but an echo, I think.'

'Echoes, alas! are all I can achieve,' said Henry. 'I suppose you read lots of poetry; and write it, too, I daresay. And here we are at the kitchen garden. May I savour its delights by pinching everything? . . . Lavender, bay, lemon-mint, thyme, sage. . . . Delicious! And, look, a moss-rose! banished from its proper terrain. One hardly ever sees a moss-rose nowadays.'

'Would you like one?' she said, and picked a bud, which she handed to him rather doubtfully.

He put it into his buttonhole. Seeing it there, under his formidable jaw, she thought: 'One shouldn't give little trusting flowers to young men whose minds are a closed book to one.'

'I feel awfully proud,' said Henry. 'Do you know what I shall be saying to myself all day? *Ursula Halliday has given me a rose.*'

'I think you are still being superior; but in a different way. You have to be polite to me in my own garden, I suppose; but let me tell you, Henry, I haven't forgotten all the years of my childhood. Here are the plums, an old tree, but good enough for bottling. Mother couldn't have meant you to have the Victorias.'

'The years of your childhood? I remember three little girls, two fair and one dark—rather disconcerting little girls who used to stare at one with round, solemn eyes. But I don't know what you mean by "superior."'

'You were so haughty and aloof, I admired you from afar. I didn't really expect you to ask me to dance; but it would have been a kind thing to do. You see,' said Ursula, 'what happens to one in childhood is so very important. A slight can leave a mark for life. It can make you feel that you are a born wallflower and had better stay away from balls.'

Henry looked solemnly before him. Two little plum trees were reflected in his eyes that had never permitted miniature Ursulas to walk through their glassy gates.

'How could I have guessed that such a remote little being was suffering on my account? Is that why your attitude towards me has been so—shall we say, uncordial, since you grew up?'

'No, it isn't; and it hasn't,' said Ursula. 'Naturally, one is a little awkward with a superior person. One dries up when people think their thoughts are above one's head. And this morning you have been mocking me. But do not imagine that I mind. Because, you know, something happened, and you ceased to be a hero.'

'It was an honour that I dreamed not of. But what,' asked Henry, 'opened your eyes to the sad truth?'

'That is a thing I would rather die than tell. I was disillusioned,' said Ursula; 'and that, too, left its mark. I shall always have the feeling that one never knows about people; they may have a side to them that one wouldn't like at all.'

'This is a very serious thing,' said Henry. 'You are worrying me very much. What could it have been? I am searching my conscience, but can find nothing *you* could possibly know of. Looking back on my past, it even seems to me singularly blameless. as pasts go. I hope I am not going to be the cause of your electing to live in single blessedness.' He cocked an eyebrow at her, quizzically, with a faint smile floating precariously on his long, pale, solemn face.

'I don't know,' said Ursula, with a pensive far-away look. Her pupils contracted to little black specks in her hazel eyes, she seemed to be looking through Henry at some far-off vista.

'I think you are like a little page plucking the strings of a lute in the golden days,' said Henry softly, considering her with his head on one side.

'Life—it should be beautiful right through, like a rose,' said Ursula, not heeding him, 'like the moon,' she said. That was what she had tried to put into her picture, the rose of beauty in the heart, 'if there should be anyone who knows that . . .'

'How will you be sure that he does?' asked Henry, with a rather compassionate look on his face.

Ursula, turning her attention to him, caught this look, which was a strange one to her, and wondered what it could mean.

'This morning,' she said, 'I thought I had a touch-stone. I was feeling rather—*exaltée*—and all that. I thought I would know if a person was my kind of person. But, perhaps, after all, it wouldn't be a test.' She sighed. 'Goodness, we haven't picked a single plum,' she said.

'Ursula Halliday has given me a rose; but she has also given me two riddles to solve. I shan't get a wink of sleep tonight,' said Henry Potter.

They were returning with a full basket, when Mrs. Halliday tapped on the morning-room window.

'I want a word with you, Henry,' she called.

So they went into the white Palladian house, that had a golden tinge that summer morning, like a yellowing pearl, and smelt inside of sweet peas, and of peaches being stewed for luncheon, and on into the morning-room.

'Will you tell your mother . . .' began Mrs. Halliday. But Ursula didn't hear what Henry was to tell his mother.

Her picture had been found and put on the chimney-piece. It was there, in full view of everybody, like a precious secret of the heart shouted from the housetops.

'Where did I put that letter? It must be in the dining-room,' said Mrs. Halliday. 'Wait! I must find it.' She bustled out in her distracted way.

'Hullo! Who painted this?' said Henry, going up to the chimney-piece.

'Don't say what you think of it!' cried Ursula, putting out her hands as though to ward off something.

He turned a surprised face towards her, and opened his mouth to speak.

'Please! I'm—I'm—not prepared yet. It might be—very upsetting,' she said, standing on one foot, as if poised for flight.

'But . . .' began Henry. 'What is it, Ursula? Are you afraid I may not like it. Is that it?' he asked, gently.

She shook her head. 'I am afraid, Henry,' she said, 'that you may.'

'Turns into Yellow Gold His Salt Green Streams'

K ATHERINE SWALLOW was secretly praying that the young man, whose dark eyes kept stealing to her across the table, would not like her too much. And why should he, indeed? She was no pink-and-white beauty. There was no gold in her hair.

She was a thin, brown girl whose hair refused to curl, whose eyes, one grey, the other brown, gave her such a peculiar look that gentlemen looked askance at her. Or so she had always fancied.

The afternoon sun shed a greenish light through the thick bottle-glass of the window-panes. His head was outlined against this luminous background, beyond which—a blur of young gold, a blur of white—the poplars in the garden and a snowy pear-tree bore witness to the spring.

He had a pale triangular face, with somewhat irregular features, and eyes so dark that it seemed as if he must have a smoky vision; as if pale and delicate colours would be imperceptible to orbs so black.

One could not tell from that Puckish, enigmatical face whether he were a likeable person (and by a likeable person, she meant one to whom she could talk without being thought a queer fish, whose laughter would never shock her, but chime with her own). But the long pointed chin that jutted over his ruff disquieted her.

She had guessed what matters were afoot when her mother had commanded her that morning to wear her new satin gown, since Sir Colin Knowles was bidden to dinner. They were making yet another effort to get her a husband.

She was nineteen years old and her maidenhood a reproach. But since there was something curst in her nature which refused to accept the values of her elders and betters, the cause of her mother's chagrin, her father's displeasure, was to her a secret satisfaction. She had nothing of the allure that had betrayed her sister. Dance—poor, lovely Dance! who had been constrained to become a bride at the age of fifteen and had been sharing a great four-poster bed these two years past with a strange bearded gentleman. Dance had written her privily—'I had thought Love was a winged Sperrit, but 'tis of all things the most carnal. A mighty queer business.'

Katherine had burned the little smudged letter to ashes in her candle-flame and had thanked the Lord for her different eyes, her angular body, for everything that made her an unpalatable morsel for the sweet tooth of neighbouring squires. She liked them not!

Sometimes she thought that she had antennae as delicate as an insect's to warn her of peril. As if she had touched his mind with invisible feelers, she knew that this strange young man was not listening to her father's talk, that he was answering him only with the tip of his tongue, as it were, while his thoughts were occupied with the girl across the table—herself.

'You are not what other men would choose; but I am a perverse fellow. An't please you, I would consider your points.'

And if by some strange chance he were to take a fancy to the oddity she was, neither he nor her father would brook a denial. That masterful chin told her that he was a man who got what he wanted.

Katherine's cheeks grew hot. The smell of food and wine was overpowering. The table was in disarray, the pewter tankards set awry amid a litter of broken bread and spilt salt. There were grease spots on the polished oak round the great baron of beef that Master Swallow had lately carved. He had drunk too much canary, and was quoting Ovid to impress the young man, his eyes suffused with the tears of immoderate laughter and a knowing look on his face, as if he thought that they were secure in their secret masculine world from feminine compulsion ... Sir Colin was laughing, too, but it was the laughter of politeness and had a hollow sound. He was not at the moment interested in bawdy talk.

Mistress Swallow sat facing her husband with an array of sweetmeats before her, withdrawn into her shell, following some private train of thought. Now and again she raked her red pyramid of hair with a jewelled forefinger, cleared her throat, or heaved her bosom within its restricting corselet. One could tell by her little sniff when she was belatedly scoring an imaginary point against one of her gossips—probably Lady Ashbee, who had just married off her sixth daughter—or perhaps recollecting an actual triumph in a battle of words. Yes, she lived in a private, bustling, fussy world of her own, which bore but little resemblance, Katherine suspected, to reality.

Now and again she emerged from her shell to press more food on the guest in a false Court voice, to bring her daughter to his notice with some counterfeit word of praise for her singing, her housewifery, or other virtue. She had big ears weighed down with pearls, cold little pale-green eyes and small short-fingered hands that could deal a ringing box on the ear of an offender. Katherine remembered one such blow that had drawn blood with a clawed ring.

'Who would bid,' she said, angrily, 'for such a bag of tricks!'

But Katherine had a trick or two of which they knew nothing. She could muffle herself in a cloak of insensibility and exist within it like a chrysalis in its cocoon, refusing all contact with a world that had become too unpleasant to bear. At other times, when nothing occurred to disturb the even tenor of the days and life seemed on the surface no more than a matter of eating and sleeping and the performance of trivial household duties, she could find ecstasy in ways never suspected by those about her. In scribbling, for instance.

Having devoured in secret all the books in her father's library, merry and lewd tales and some so pranked with conceits that she grew impatient with the authors and called them foppish and strutting fellows who marred God's truth with antics, and others which so stank of the charnel-house that she refused to read further, she had been thrown back on herself, and had discovered that she was a kind of spider and could spin out of herself the web of dreams. She needed but her quill and inkhorn and the bundle of yellowish paper she had chanced upon in an old chest. But she was not content for long to spin easily and lightly out of her brain. It was as if with the persistent scratching of her quill, she had scratched her way through to some deeper place, the existence of which she had never suspected.

Whatever it might be, that mysterious reservoir of dreams, she knew that when she got through to it, things happened that were out of her control. The characters in her tales became alive and spoke with voices she could hear as clearly as those of real persons. They had thoughts separate from her own which she could not always fathom, and they acted as she had not foreseen they would act.

When the writing fit was on her, she lived a kind of double existence—one upon the surface of the earth and the other somewhere beyond space and time. She stole what she valued from the surface life to embalm in the other—golden and silver poplars dancing in the wind; the first star of evening, that shines in the green of the west when the rosy islands have faded to ashes; the smell of the earth after rain.

'I have writ that which no man hath ever writ. For Woman is Water that catcheth the reflections of things. She is Air that stealeth odours sweet from bud and herb. But Man is Earth and Fire.' So she scribbled on a margin, thinking that when poets spoke of flowers it was to compare them to the beauties of a mistress and never for the flower's sweet sake. Not one of them, it seemed, so loved a rose that it made a rose of his heart.

And seizing a fresh sheet, she dipped her quill and tried her hand at poetry—

> Shall I to a rose my love compare,
>   Who is but flesh and bone?
> He hath no charm to take the air.
>   With breath of petals blown.
>
> When I to his heart my sorrows take
>   What comfort shall I find?
> He hath no dew my thirst to slake,
>   No honey for my mind . . .
>
> He is but a man as others are,
>   For worms predestined meat.
> But tryst keep I with dusk's green star
>   And go on wingèd feet.

Oh, dear! what stuff! And she had inked her fingers and spoiled a fair sheet. If she were a man, poetry, she supposed, would have dripped from her pen as naturally as rain from a cloud. So far as she knew, letters were a purely masculine accomplishment. Dance had written that many of the young men who visited at her house in London wrote sonnets and odes which were handed round from one to another, and that one of them, 'a very personable young gentleman, who hath a Spanish cast of countenance, hath writ a satire on London Town that is much talked of ... but it hath no loves or doves, nor other sweet rhymes, and falleth harshly on my little ears.'

'Little ears.' That was just like Dance who was aware of all her good points and tender towards them—though she had small cause to be, since thanks to them the elderly Master Challinor had cast covetous eyes on her, and got her against her will.

Now that her old pedagogue was dead, there was no one in all the world, thought Katherine, to whom she would dare to show her writings. He had taught her Latin and many other things, and was responsible, perhaps, for some of her queerness. He used to say that she was the best pupil he ever had—except one. And that was a boy long ago at the Grammar School, no scholar, but a born understander, one that could give you back what you told him with something added of his own, something that turned plain fact into cold magic. The Lord knew how! ''Twas as if dry-as-dust had been dipped in a moonbeam. God 'ild him, I fear he hath come to a bad end.'

It was thanks to her old pedagogue that Katherine knew more Latin than her father suspected. She was afraid that her crimson cheeks would give her away to those appraising dark eyes across the table and was glad when Master Swallow began to talk of his recent visit to Court and the Queen's Majesty.

'And did you kiss her hand, father?' she asked, breaking the silence that had been imposed upon her.

'I kissed her diamonds, poppet. Her sainted flesh was not for these unworthy lips. God's grace, you could not see so much as a knuckle for gems. Even her teeth are pearls of the rarer kind—for they are black. Ha, ha, ha.'

'And you, sir, you have been often at Court?' asked Mistress Swallow.

'But half-a-dozen times in all. I am no courtier, save by necessity. I have but lately returned, you know, from the Low Countries to claim my patrimony. But London hath me in a thrall. I saw a play at the Rose the other night so charmed me that I am yet a little bewitched. It was a piece about fairies, gossamer stuff but very well knit. There was a line in it—I know not why, it seems to me the most beautiful I have ever heard . . .'

He dropped his voice as he said the last words, as if he half regretted speaking of a matter that was too intimate.

And suddenly it seemed to Katherine that something wonderful had happened—as if she had seen a falling star drop soundlessly down the steeps of space. Their eyes met again across the table, and this time, for some strange reason, they exchanged a smile—a fleeting, secret smile that was like a signal between two spies from some far country.

Mrs. Swallow rose at this moment, and Sir Colin sprang to his feet to open the door for the ladies. His long thin hand on the latch, with a deep scar across the knuckles, caught Katherine's eye, and she felt an almost irresistible impulse to touch it with her own. Whence came that queer unwarrantable desire, she knew not. It took her completely by surprise and disquieted her.

To escape from her thoughts she went out into the garden and watched for a while the gardener trimming the knots, which made a pattern like an Eastern carpet below the terrace. Soon the white pear tree in the kitchen garden beckoned her away. A starling whistled out of its drifts of snow, his body glistening like dark shot-silk in the April sunlight. There was a warm, delicious scent of wallflowers. Grey and silver herbs; the weather-stained roof of the barn that had a purplish bloom like ripe plums; young heart-shaped poplar-leaves that are never still, but dance with every air that blows; she drew them consciously into her mind and stored them away. Beyond the gate in the nut-hedge, a ploughed field, delicate, fawn-coloured and ribbed like corduroy, stretched down to the wood.

She glanced back at the house with its twisted chimneys. A

puff of blue smoke spread fanwise against the sky . . . a deeper, softer blue than the clear turquoise to which it mounted. One of the panes of the library window was flashing like a diamond. In that rather musty room with its black-lettered tomes, its great carved mantel from which the bust of Julius Cæsar looked into space, its green-leaved tapestry of Angers, her father was probably at this moment closeted with the guest—twitting him, perhaps, with nods and winks and gusts of wheezy laughter, because there was no mistress yet for the great house at Wyvernhoe which Sir Colin had just inherited.

'Pest!' said Katherine, aloud, 'I will not think on't.' And turning her back on the house, she picked up her sprigged petticoats and climbed over the gate.

The wood was waiting, green and cool and secret, with a strange intensity, as of having been abandoned in haste by some supernatural being. She seemed to hear a sighing—'Hush . . . sh . . . sh!' whispered from tree to tree, through the undergrowth and down the glades as her skirts rustled over the mast of last year's dead leaves.

The wood held its breath lest a mortal should surprise its ghostly visitant; a blackbird frantically uttered its warning; a pheasant rose with a clatter of wings, and rabbits bolted for cover.

In a clearing there was a golden willow-palm, set about with nests of primroses. Oh, God, what beauty! She went down on her knees and began to gather the primroses, heaping them in her lap. There is something very delicate and touching about the scent of a primrose. It is like the compassion of a robin, that will suddenly burst into a wild, sweet stave when your heart is breaking. Flower and bird, they seem to be telling you—'My all is but a thimbleful, but what I have, I give you.'

But when one was dying, thought Katherine, it might be that one would forget the passions and the glories and remember of Life only some minute consolation, such as these.

A brook gurgled somewhere out of sight. When she had made a bunch of the primroses, encircled them with soft furry leaves and bound them with a ribbon from her sleeve, she went to look for the brook.

And suddenly in the next clearing she came upon a man seated on the trunk of a fallen tree.

At the first glance, she thought Sir Colin must have got here before her; for he was dressed in a suit of black and had the air of a city man.

But it was not Sir Colin.

Having been brought up to mistrust profoundly strange gallants, and solemnly admonished never to walk abroad unattended Katherine turned to flee, caught her foot in a root, and fell sprawling all her length.

'Pest!' said the stranger, in a startled tone of voice. 'You have scattered my thoughts, madam, to all the airs of April.'

He rose and picked her up.

'Lord, what a mess!' he said, in a pleasant voice, that had a country burr in it, and producing a handkerchief, he proceeded to wipe the mud off her skirts.

He was a thickset fellow, large-eyed as a hare, with a high forehead and little gold rings in his ears.

'I crave your pardon, sir, I fear you have spoiled your kerchief. As for your thoughts, you must e'en whistle them back again,' said Katherine, suddenly light-hearted, and ashamed of her momentary panic. This man wouldn't hurt a fly.

'You must have green thoughts,' she went on, with her little tinkling laugh, 'who use so green a closet. I had thought myself alone in this wood.'

'And were frighted to come on mortal grossness, where you had a tryst with some winged thing. Is it not so?'

'Perhaps,' said she. 'Indeed, methought I heard the rustle of feathered heels. But you came to study, sir, and I disturb you.' For her eye had fallen on an inkhorn balanced precariously on the fallen log, and a quarto sheet covered with a black, spidery script was lying at her feet. He stooped to pick up the sheet and stowed it away in his pocket.

'The mischief is done, madam,' he said. 'But blame not yourself. You have as much right to this wood as I; though I doubt we are both interlopers.'

'I came here to find peace,' she said. 'Oh, my primroses, they are all muddied o'er.'

'We will wash them in the brook. And my kerchief, too. See, they are restored to their pristine beauty, and the kerchief will be dry anon.' He hung it on an alder twig.

' 'Tis of a rare colour,' said Katherine, and an idea suddenly occurring to her—'its device of strawberries hath something ... it maketh of it such a kerchief as would serve in a tale for a love-token.' The pupils of her eyes dilated, and she turned to him excitedly. There was something so gentle and understanding in his smile that she was emboldened to proceed, a little breathlessly and with the faint rose-colour coming and going in her olive cheeks—'I would have a faithless lover come upon it— oh! long after he had forgot his mistress. And I would have him pierced to the core with the sudden memory of his lost love. Oh! but he should be smitten to the heart, remembering some little trick she had, or a brown freckle on her left eyelid, or what not.'

'And would he hold her again in his arms, to the sound of marriage-bells? Would Comedy be your vein?'

'Ah, no!' said Katherine. 'For he would not deserve to have her. Love doth not recover from a wound so deep, and she would have none of him.'

'Then would she be no true woman, that set her pride so higher than her love.'

'Think you so? You have studied the nature of woman, sir, that you speak with such an air of authority?'

'I know not where I got the knowledge, mistress. But it is mine,' he said. 'Perhaps my trade hath taught it me.'

'Your trade? Then you *are* a writer?' she asked eagerly.

'A poor scribbler, madam—a play-actor by profession.'

'I like not our modern writers—such as I have read—save only *The Defence of Poesie* and *The Shepheard's Calendar*. But the *Eclogues* of Virgil please me mightily, for there is much of pastoral in them. If I were a poet, I would write of little unconsidered things ... of these primroses, for instance, that are so sweet. If there be words so delicate and of such fairy breath to catch their essence.'

He took the bunch from her and put it to his lips.

'So faint,' he said, 'and tender. They know not the heat of the sun. Aye, there are words for them. One has but to reach out one's hand and take them from the air.'

Something in the words, in the sound of his voice as he uttered them, sent a shiver down her spine, as though an icy finger had touched her.

'You said you came here to find peace. What troubleth you, child? Come, let us sit upon this log and talk. I know not what wind blew you hither, but I think it was the sweet South that hath the odour of violets.'

'I would ask you a question. I could ask it of no other in the world. Prithee, tell me, have I a face could take a man's fancy?'

'You are no Greekish beauty,' he said consideringly, his hare's eyes lingering on her irregular features and tapering chin. 'But a man might take such a liking to your heretic face, that grows in grace with looking, as to find it one day carved upon his heart— like an intaglio cut into stone. And hath he come, and have you run from him? What kind of man is he that you should fear his love?'

'I know not. He hath a locked face, to which I have no key. Perhaps he liketh me not. But he looked upon me as if he would draw me down into the darkness of his eyes, only I doubt they are too jetty dark to see a thing so pale. At first I prayed he would not like me overmuch, for I had no mind to lose my freedom. But now—I know not what has come to me, but I fear I am more than half o'erthrown. 'Twas a thing he said—not meant for me. He was talking of a play he had seen—something about fairies. "There was a line in it—I think it is the most beautiful I have ever heard," he said. Doth it seem a little thing to fall in love for? But 'twas the way he said it . . . as if . . . as if . . . oh, as if a star had flashed and fallen.'

'And did he speak the line?' asked the playactor, two little pinpoints of light shining in the pupils of his eyes.

'No. I cannot think that I shall ever hear it—for now I am sure he liketh me not at all.'

'I am no soothsayer,' said the stranger, with his bright, compassionate smile, 'and yet I dare swear he is thinking on you at this very moment—"So looked she, and so smiled. I am sure she liketh me not at all; and what care I? And yet—the devil take her—she hath the most delicate, sweet face I ever looked on, the most like a flower."'

'You speak the most comfortable words that e'er I heard,' said Katherine, with a sigh.

The apricot light of sunset shone through the young beech boughs and the shadows beneath the trees were pools of amethyst, and still they talked, the damp breath of dusk bedewing their garments and chilling their hands and feet. It was not until a blackbird, uttering his startled evening cry, flew over their heads that Katherine awoke to reality. Heavens, what a pother, what a hue-and-cry there must be at home this very moment!

'Fare you well, sir. I know not what power you have, but I ne'er unlocked my heart before to mortal creature . . . What must you think of me that have told you . . . oh, I blush to think what I have told you.'

'God be with, mistress. I know not your name, nor you mine. And your secrets—why, you have dropped them into a well so deep it hath no bottom . . .'

He took her cold, thin hand and kissed it. 'When I think on you . . . I'll think on April's darling flowers . . . and call you Perdita, who art best to me.' And then, with a sudden change of tone, he added irrelevantly, 'I would I knew what line it was he liked so much . . .'

Spade Man from over the Water

M RS. ASHER was having tea with Mrs. Penny when the telegram came. She was leaning back, with her two long feet on the fender, talking and waving her lovely hands, that seemed to go about with her like attendant doves and to lead an independent existence, swooping and perching in gestures that dramatized her share of the conversation and made even her chance remarks sound significant. They settled to rest on her knee when Mrs. Penny opened the telegram, but rose and fluttered towards that lady when she uttered a little cry.

'My husband! He'll be home on Friday,' said Mrs. Penny, looking suddenly transparent with happiness.

'My dear, I do so rejoice with you,' said Mrs. Asher, recalling her hands, that had seemed to wish to bear her joy straight into Mrs. Penny's breast.

'I wonder . . . Oh, Mrs. Asher, I do hope that you and he will be great friends!'

Mrs. Asher's dark eyes went to a photograph on the mantelpiece. 'I know *I* shall like *him*,' she said. 'He looks everything that your husband should be . . . So *kind*,' she said, giving the word a sonorous quality that made kindness into a rare and knightly virtue, 'and *fastidious* . . . and *sensitive*.' As if she were playing a little tune, she emphasized each adjective on her knee with a different finger. 'Proud, too,' she added. 'Oh, there is integrity in that face! One would trust him on sight.'

'But,' cried Mrs. Penny, with a look of dismay, 'that isn't Rupert! It's a cousin of mine, Arnold Cross. He's a dear, as you say, but not the very least like my husband. Whatever made you . . . ? I can't think how such a mistake could have come about.'

She was profoundly shocked. Mrs. Asher, that understanding woman, to have been entertaining all this time so erroneous an idea! Why, if she herself were to meet Mrs. Asher's two little boys in the street, she would recognize them instinctively. She knew by sympathy exactly what they were like. She liked Mrs. Asher so much, she seemed to know her husband too; though he had never been mentioned between them.

Mrs. Asher had a deep sense of tragedy, as people have whose sense of humour is very keen. That was what made her so precious as a friend. Having once found her, you couldn't bear the thought of ever losing her. She was, like poetry, one of the things that do not fail. If the loss of Mr. Asher had stricken her so deeply that she could not speak of him, it was because she was of heroic stature and had to drain to the dregs the cup that lesser mortals dare only to sip. Mr. Asher, Laura Penny was convinced, was like Charles Lamb—Mrs. Asher's favourite writer. He must have hated dying and going off into the dark without her.

'Oh, Mrs. Asher!' said Laura, 'I thought you would have known that Rupert is ... well, a very *magnetic* kind of person. I still sometimes think that it's all a dream, my being married to him. Isn't it absurd—after nearly a year?'

Mrs. Asher looked about her in a hunted kind of way. But there was no other photograph in the room.

'Oh, dear!' she said, 'and I thought I saw the marriage likeness between you, as the gipsies say. He looks,' she said, 'like the man you *ought* to have married. But, never mind! I must readjust my ideas.' She twisted her mouth in that expressive way that seemed to make it the seat of her emotions, and added, laughing, 'I suppose you really married the Spade man from over the water!'

Laura gave a little start. A dark man from over the water ... a stranger. He had walked into the hotel in Bloomsbury to which she had gone, all lost and bewildered, when her father had died and left her, entangled like a desiccated fly in the abandoned web of his existence. Her father had been paralysed for ten years, and she had had to be paralysed too, all the time, every minute of the day. Even now, sometimes, she groped in the night for her dressing-gown, dreaming that she heard the remorseless thumping of his stick.

And then memory came flooding back, and she sank into the

pillows as into a rosy cloud. Being loved by Rupert made you feel as beautiful as Helen of Troy. He had the darkest, most shining eyes in the world, and when he looked at you, you felt as helpless as a rose rifled by bees.

Oh, it was very odd that so intuitive a person had not felt the rare quality of Rupert's charm! One couldn't speak of him in just an ordinary voice, because to mention his name was to hear the sound of trumpets, to smell red clove carnations, to feel a warmth as of wine in one's veins.

Mrs. Asher's past might lie beyond a closed door. She might have come into one's life as down a long corridor of time, but she had brought her memories with her. They were behind her eyes, looking out of them, and in the tones of her voice, causing vibrations like those of a bell when its peal has died on the air. One felt her memories like a presence. Soon Laura was thinking of Mr. Asher as a person she had known in the flesh. She imagined them as so much part of one another that they could answer each other's unspoken thoughts, their love so deeply rooted that he could drop a kiss on that delicate hollowed cheek of hers without disturbing her thoughts. He was the sort of man who would bring her the first white violets, or a dead bee, or a young fir-cone; and she the sort of woman to run to his study crying, 'Charles (was that his name, after all?), listen to this poem I came across'; or 'Charles, come quickly and see the light in the sky.'

Would the time ever come for Laura to be unaware of Rupert's kiss? To think her own thoughts in his presence as tranquilly as if he were the air she breathed? Or would he always make her feel in his arms as if the world had spun away from beneath her feet? Would she ever meet that dark, mocking gaze without a shyness that was exquisite pain? 'So prim,' he said, with the chuckle that seemed to come from unplumbed depths of humour in him, 'and chilly, like a snowdrop. It always was my favourite flower.'

There had been a break in the continuity of her existence. It was almost as if Rupert had created a new Laura. Drawn into his orbit, one could but revolve dizzily round him in the void. She had lost touch with her past self. She was wildly happy, but there was this queer feeling of disintegration.

It was Mrs. Asher who gave her back the self she had lost, the self that first her father and then her husband had filched from her, the Laura who had loved to be alone to think her thoughts, to dance to the tunes she heard in her mind. For Mrs. Asher was as good as solitude. Laura could hardly have paid her a greater compliment. It was strange that so restless and nervous a person should create so deep a tranquillity about her. All Mrs. Asher's tricks, her gesticulating hands, the twisting of her mobile mouth, the way she was always losing things and having to search for them, but served to emphasize the sense of inward peace one felt in her company.

She had moved into the house over the way on the very day that Rupert went abroad. He had allowed Laura to choose the country to live in because the nature of his work took him away quite often, but he hadn't let her have the empty house she had fallen in love with—a tip-tilted black-and-white cottage, with the date 1590 carved into the lintel and the intriguing name 'Miss Lemon's Cottage' painted on the gate.

'Too dilapidated. And damp, I shouldn't wonder. It's been empty for years,' he said, 'and nobody's likely to take it, thank God! Fields on either side and a derelict house opposite—what could be better! No one to run in and out—a thing I can't stand. Why, we could play at Adam and Eve in our garden, and not a soul to spy. Besides, your home is in my heart . . . isn't it, isn't it?'

So they settled into their modern house, and she made it very fresh and gay with cretonnes and limed oak from Heals's to match its newness. On the days he went to London, the house seemed strangely empty—like a beach when the tide goes out. When he returned, it glowed and sang, as if life had come pouring back into it.

Mrs. Asher came over to borrow some matches. She looked terribly tired. Her furniture was standing in the road, amidst the litter of straw and sacking disgorged by the pantechnicon. The pieces looked forlorn, as if they felt the wrench from the past and were suffering in the east wind. Looking at them, one felt a little dubious of Mrs. Asher's good taste. No Chippendale, no elegance.

But one's heart went out to her instantly, as it might go out to a giraffe at the Zoo because of its limpid eyes and its awkward grace.

'You've taken the house I'd set my heart on,' said Laura.

'Then, please, make it yours,' Mrs. Asher said, with a queenly gesture. 'Please run in and out as you like.'

How trusting and generous, thought Laura, with a little pang, remembering Rupert's prejudices. He had only just quitted the house. It seemed still to vibrate with his presence. She hadn't had time to look into the abyss of the three months' parting that yawned at her feet.

Mrs. Asher gave her no time.

'Come and help me,' she said, as if to an old friend.

And in a little while, 'Miss Lemon's Cottage' seemed as much Laura's as Mrs. Asher's.

It was extraordinary the way the heavy mahogany snuggled into it with an effect of integrity and permanence, an air of being valued not for aesthetic reasons, but for something that had to do with the heart's affections. The house was one in which light bloomed softly like a great golden rose. The smell of newly-baked bread and roses greeted one's nostrils, even though the year was too old for roses, and the incongruous things in the drawing-room achieved a harmony that was completely satisfying, because of Mrs. Asher's instinct for reconciling one colour with another, one period with another, by placing in juxtaposition to the discordant elements some object that beautifully resolved their differences.

'I shall live and die here,' she said, with a contented sigh. 'There will never be any reason to move again.'

In the chances and changes of life with a rover like Rupert, it was comforting to think that 'Miss Lemon's Cottage' would always be there, with its golden light and its quintessence of rose.

She had come, Mrs. Asher said, because of the ancient Grammar School. Her little boys were at boarding-school till the end of term, but next term they would live with her and go to the Grammar School.

'Oh dear!' she said, coming upon a small, very dirty eiderdown in a chest. 'Here is Gavin's downie, his totem-rag. He couldn't bear to be parted from it, couldn't sleep, or come downstairs, or face strangers without hugging his downie. I suppose it gave him a feeling of protection. I must give it a good wash and put it on his bed,' she said, her eyes lit with tenderness.

Somehow, Laura couldn't mention Mrs. Asher in her letters. She knew very well how irksome Rupert would find the thought of a woman on his doorstep, and one, moreover, who was wholly unaccustomed to the idea of intrusion. It would be better, she thought, to break to him gently the astonishing fact that in his absence she had formed a friendship which would last as long as life lasted.

Not that she would put it like that, of course. Rupert's mind was still an unexplored country. Once she dreamed of being lost in the dark in some strange landscape and of hearing a sound of gurgling water. 'That's Rupert's laughter; but I don't know where it comes from,' she cried in her dream. She felt a terrible urgency to find the source of the chuckling water, and set off on one of those perilous and futile dream-journeys, when one's legs seem weighted with lead and intangible obstacles block one's path. When she woke, the dream seemed to have lasted all night. It left her feeling physically exhausted and a little frightened.

The truth was that Rupert didn't really like people; though people fell for him . . . old ladies in hotels and young women in the train, and tradesmen and bus-conductors and charwomen.

'Your starchy Cheltenham relations—let's keep them at arm's length,' he said. And when Arnold Cross sent that photograph from India—'Good Lord, what a prig! So long as he stays in Delhi and doesn't come bothering us . . .'

From the depths of her armchair, little Mrs. Penny looked at Mrs. Asher consideringly, the colour coming and going in her cheeks. She was trying to see her friend with Rupert's eyes. It was terrible—like seeing a distorted reflection in a train window which bestows a foreknowledge of the friend beside you in extreme old age, or even in death. And then, as you turn with relief to the contemporary, the real, face, Laura saw once more the face of *her* Mrs. Asher, and vowed to herself that neither Rupert nor any other force should come between them.

The winter afternoon had closed in. The sky still held a watery yellow light, faint as primroses, and pools of heliotrope shadow lay under the trees. The withered bines of the clematis on the wall were ropes of silver. In the myrtle bush beyond the window a ghost fire was fantastically burning. How lovely! And there was the back view of a ghostly Mrs. Asher sitting on the frosty grass, like Keats's ghostly queen of spades. ('A Spade man from over the water', she had said, with her little hollow laugh.)

Mrs. Asher was still looking pensively at Arnold's photograph, her chin cupped in her hand. But probably her thoughts were far away.

'Wait!' said Laura. 'I have a snapshot of us on our honeymoon, feeding the pigeons in Venice.'

She got up and searched in a drawer.

'Here it is!'

She handed the bit of pasteboard to her friend with an expectant look, as if she were waiting for a little sound of surprise.

'It's getting dark. I must take it to the window,' Mrs. Asher said, rising in her leisurely way.

'We'll have the light,' Laura put out her hand to the switch, but on Mrs. Asher's protesting that she loved the twilight, she poked the fire instead.

Mrs. Asher's tall, straight figure at the window quenched the fire in the myrtle bush. The warmth and cosiness inside were no longer projected into the grey and silver world without. The light had died in the sky and a greenish star shone, faint as a glow-worm, over the thin black poplar.

Mrs. Asher seemed to be peering at the snapshot as if she couldn't quite see.

'As I'm to meet him at Greenock,' said Laura, waiting, 'I suppose I shall be away a couple of days.'

'Yes,' said Mrs. Asher, turning at last. 'No doubt you will want to spend a night in London. He is a very handsome man, my dear.' She gave her soft little laugh. 'No wonder you were surprised at my . . . *absurd* mistake!'

She gathered her furs about her, stooped, and for the first time kissed Laura's cheek. She was not a demonstrative woman, and a kiss from her was as sweet and surprising as a gift of chill Christmas roses.

Laura caught her hands. 'Oh, my dear, how glad I am that Fate sent you my way! But you're not going yet? Do have another cup of tea.'

'You must have much to do. And so have I,' said Mrs. Asher.

Yes, of course; she was expecting the boys home. How nice that Mrs. Asher, too, had happiness to look forward to.

She would like Rupert, of course. Oh, everyone had to succumb to that compelling charm of his! And he? If one were very tactful, if one didn't rush things, if one let her dawn on him, as it were, gradually, oh! surely Rupert would take to her unique, her delightful Mrs. Asher. Laura wouldn't, at first, say a word. Indeed, she knew very well that her thoughts would be too much in a whirl, and for him alone.

But, as they approached 'Miss Lemon's Cottage,' he might notice, perhaps, that it was inhabited. Golden light would be shining out through the curtains, smoke coming from the chimneys. 'Hullo!' he might say. 'So the house opposite has been let.'

That would be her chance. 'Yes,' she would reply, in a light, unconcerned voice; 'but to a quiet, unassuming kind of person —a Mrs. Asher. You'd like her, I think.'

But when the time came there was no golden light, no smoke. 'Miss Lemon's Cottage' was as dark as the tomb, as hollow as a forsaken nest. A house-agent's sign creaked in the wind. Some wisps of straw were blown to Laura's feet, then lifted and whirled away with a faint rustling, like a desolate word whispered in the ear. 'Treachery,' her lips repeated soundlessly, over and over again, 'treachery, treachery.'

'But whose?' asked a little, lost, cold voice from nowhere.

Strings in Hollow Shells

'IT's divine to be here again,' Sandra said, tossing her pill-box of a hat on to a table and burying her face in a bowl of roses. She seemed to be eating them with her greedy carmine lips. 'I'm so tah'd, Mrs. Prideaux. I don't think I've ever been so tah'd in my life. God knows why one lives in London, when there's all this.' She opened her arms to the view, as if she would gather it to her breast. 'Oh, those hills!' she said, 'and the larch-wood, and the pattern of the fields like a Paisley shawl.'

'Have some tea,' said Mrs. Prideaux, drily.

'Nothing has changed,' said Sandra, looking about her. She knew the room so well, the shiny white walls with a shinier satin stripe in the paper, the shiny chintz, the pewter and lustre jugs on the chimneypiece, the faded water-colours—a pleasant, rather characterless country-house drawing-room, with a patterned carpet and fat armchairs.

'To think,' she said, stroking her delicate arched brows with a pink-tipped finger, as if to smooth away some small twitching pain, a trick of hers, 'how much water has flowed under bridges since I was last here!'

There was one person in the room who interpreted correctly the implications of her remark. He knew, the unobtrusive person in the background who had not yet been introduced, that what she had really said was—'How I have lived and suffered, while you have been existing tranquilly in your backwater!'

Indeed, her next words were—'What I love about Closters is that nothing ever seems to happen here. One feels so safe . . . like coming home to haven from the high seas.'

'Except love and birth and death,' said Mrs. Prideaux, crisply, 'the usual adventures. After all, the house has been standing for two hundred years.'

'But it has such an atmosphere of tranquillity. Good, peaceful people have lived here. No one has died at Closters of a broken heart, no one has been betrayed or forsaken. Oh, I *know!*' said Sandra. 'I am very sensitive to atmosphere. The very smell in the hall as one comes in—I don't know what it is, but it's been there ever since I was a child, like the Doré engraving and the red lacquer cabinet and your golf-cape on a peg, a smell of new wool, like fresh fluffy blankets, and wood-smoke and camphor—so comforting. When something *appalling* happens, one's natural instinct is to turn to Closters.'

'Appalling?' said Mrs. Prideaux. 'My dear, I hope not.'

'Oh, I don't know. I seem to be a person things happen to.' Sandra's eyes were dark with her mysterious sorrow. 'Not that I wear my heart on my sleeve, or anything like that. I'm pretty tough, really. Let's not talk about me. I just *adore* being here.'

'There's nothing like a nice cup of tea after a journey, I always think,' said another figure in the background, making her first effort to project herself into Miss Pellew's consciousness. 'I don't suppose you know who I am.'

'Oh, don't you know Etta—my sister-in-law?' said Mrs. Prideaux, surprised. 'And my cousin Simon, Mr. Hart? I am so sorry. I always imagine that people have met before.'

Sandra's eyes flickered over them, while her face wore its vacant look.

'I don't remember,' she said, vaguely.

'I've never known anyone forget Simon. People ask after him years later. And sometimes I hear that he is getting letters from people he has met here who have long ceased to write to me. And yet he is a dry sarcastic man—rather a brute,' said Mrs. Prideaux, smiling tenderly at Mr. Hart, who sat looking at the toes of his shoes with an inscrutable expression.

'Really?' said Sandra, uninterested.

'Men are two a penny to her,' remarked Etta to her other self, catching at a loop with her crochet hook. She named a certain fashion paper to herself, referring not to Sandra's clothes, which were modish enough, but to that expression of ennui and faint disdain which, even more than their exquisitely tailored suits, their pearls and sables, proclaims the sophistication of fashion models, and vaguely suggests, to such as Etta, unplumbable depths of worldly wisdom and experience.

'Have you read anything nice lately, Sandra? You must give me a list of the new books,' Mrs. Prideaux was saying.

'Darling,' said Sandra, 'I don't believe you ever read a word of anything I recommend.'

'You sent me the stories of Tchekhov for Christmas. I liked them very much. I don't know why, but they made me feel that I'd been listening to a very nice concert.'

'I think that was an inspired thing to do,' said Simon Hart, speaking for the first time. 'I can see now that Tchekhov would suit Mrs. Prideaux admirably.'

Sandra's eyes focussed on Mr. Hart. They took in a thin man with a brown bird-like face and eyes like buttons of onyx. She was surprised that he had read Tchekhov. Dickens, she thought, and perhaps Gilbert White, would be more his cup of tea. He looked like a country solicitor or something of that sort and was most probably quite abysmally dull. As for Etta, she was one of those gaunt virgins with sad, top-heavy hair that had once been beautiful and a large, empty face.

What colourless, uninteresting people Mrs. Prideaux gathered about her! But it was just as well. One didn't want to be bothered with personal relationships. One wanted a rest from all that.

One had known such wonderful people, people so rich in temperament that they seemed to cast pools of amethyst and sapphire at one's feet, like a rose-window. One wore a golden cloak in their company and pinned orchids at one's breast and walked on tip-toe. But always something happened, some cruelty, some perfidy, and one's heart was cracked in two.

'But I would rather life broke my heart than passed me by,' thought Sandra. She looked compassionately at the three other occupants of the room; at Mrs. Prideaux, particularly, who had so little self that her friends were her friends not for any affinities she felt between herself and them, but for quite other reasons—because she had known them since they were children, because their aunt had been at school with her, because she had been asked to befriend them, or merely because they were her neighbours. Their faults might exasperate her, their virtues win her approval, but neither eventually affected the quality of her friendship, in which they were safely enclosed for good, as in a soft aspic-like substance, cool and impermeable. One was all of a piece to her—Sandra Pellew, an idea in her mind. Whatever she had conceived one to be in the beginning, that one remained for her. So safe, so soothing. But how pathetically unaware she was! 'Poor sweet!' thought Sandra. 'You have been married and you have lost your Herbert, but have known neither exaltation nor agony. I would rather be poor tragic little me.'

'Darling,' she said aloud, 'I'm going to play the gramophone all day in the garden and read poetry. You won't have to bother about me at all. I am going to soak myself in the view.'

She was as good as her word.

Snatches of a Beethoven quartet would come floating inter-mittently to Simon reading at a respectful distance, to Etta going about in gardening gloves and a large straw hat such as French cows wear, to Mrs. Prideaux laying flowers in a shallow basket, passing from bed to bed with a pair of secateurs.

In a cool green dress and with corals in her ears, she would descend on them, with that look on her face as of returning from another world, and be silent and *distraite,* so that both Simon and Etta were made to feel themselves in the presence of a superior being. Only Mrs. Prideaux entertained the angel unawares. 'I always think the very nicest thing one can have for tea is cucum-ber sandwiches,' she would say.

'Heavenly,' said Sandra, absent-mindedly helping herself to yet another. She ate a great many of them and somehow made the act poetical, reminding Simon of a roe or a young hart feeding among the lilies. But from his wooden face and expres-sionless eyes one would never have guessed what Simon was thinking.

'I wonder, Sandra,' said Mrs. Prideaux one day, 'if you would be very kind and receive Lucas Silverthorn for me to-morrow. His train arrives at five, and we,' she took in the other two with a smile that somehow managed to convey to them the informa-tion that although this was the first they had heard of it, she had arranged for them to take part in some project she was about to disclose—'we have to go to a bazaar at Wold. Etta is to help with the tea, Simon is in charge of the shooting-gallery—Oh, but Simon, you must! I promised, and it's too late now—and *I* am opening the bazaar. So, you see . . .' She spread out her hands palms upwards with her serene and confident smile.

Lucas Silverthorn turned out to be a tall reedy youth with flaming hair and white eyelashes.

'I'm afraid you've got rather a governessy little room,' Sandra said, flinging open the door. 'It's reserved for the young. I used to have it myself till a few years ago. But now I'm nearly thirty.'

'I don't mind. I like governesses.' Lucas looked about him. 'I like it. It rings my bell,' he said, sweeping his hand over the room and touching with antennæ-like fingers a Spanish coffer of which Mrs. Prideaux had probably forgotten the existence. Many an object of virtu blushed unseen and unpolished in odd corners of Closters, Mrs. Prideaux setting little store by the taste of by-gone Prideaux and reserving her affections for the pieces acquired through her own or her late husband's percipience.

'Books about governesses are enthralling, don't you think? I am rather a governessy sort of person myself. I am demure and say nothing, but I have my thoughts. What by the way is your name?'

'Sandra Pellew.'

'How romantic! Nearly as romantic as mine. I do hope you are staying as long as I am. Paying visits is such a strain.' He heaved a sigh and sat down on the bed.

'Oh, I don't know. When one's at a loose end. . . . And the country, of course, is quite divine. Of course, I nearly go crackers sometimes with boredom. Mrs. Prideaux is divine. I adore her. But there's no one here who talks the same language.'

'Mrs. Prideaux and my mother sewed the same sampler and all that. I never expected her to talk my language. But I'm going to like you. I've never met a woman with a heart-shaped face before. If one were a sculptor. . . .' He began to weave his preter-naturally long fingers about an imaginary bust.

Like a wolfish child which assimilates every detail of a strange face and takes it away into its private mind to gnaw, Lucas was given to dissecting the personalities of all on whom his pale gaze fell. He had his own peculiar labels for the pigeon-holes into which he tossed the results of his investigations. The most mys-terious of these pigeon-holes was one inscribed 'Byzantium'. It contained very few dossiers.

'You won't know what I mean, but Byzantine is the adjective I should choose to describe you.'

'Why wouldn't I know? I have read Yeats. He is my favourite poet.'

'But this is too thrilling!' cried Lucas, weaving his hands together. 'I am going to adore you. I have always dreamed of an inconsequent but terribly sophisticated woman into whose hands one could put one's naked heart. I like your lipstick and the French way you do your hair and the subtle scent I remark in the atmosphere.' He sniffed voluptuously and turned up his eyes.

'You absurd person! said Sandra, considering him dispassionately. 'I think you are really an orchis . . . pretending to be a human being.'

'Am I? I have always been afraid that I wasn't quite a real person,' said Lucas, sighing.

'But people like you and me who care about beauty and have an inner life are the only real ones,' said Sandra, kindly.

That evening she put on some records. 'Ondine!' said Lucas, clasping his hands. They smiled at each other like two people who share a secret. Simon Hart was playing chess by himself in a corner and seemed to be lost beyond recall in some realm of thought so remote as to be inaccessible to the rest of them, except perhaps to Mrs. Prideaux who was watching him; and Etta had abandoned her crochet for a piece of church embroidery. She knew about music, too, and intended to let them know that she had a perfect right to be included in their magic circle.

'Who is the pianist?' she asked in an interested voice, leaning forward with an intent look on her face.

'Musicky,' said Sandra, quickly, in the voice of one who gives information perfunctorily because she does not expect it to mean anything to the enquirer.

Musicky? it couldn't be. She hadn't bothered to articulate the name distinctly. But Lucas muttered 'Musicky', too, in the same sort of preoccupied voice. Nonplussed, she nodded her head wisely. It was fortunate that she didn't commit herself in any way, for when she contrived to get a look at the record, she found that the name, after all, was Gieseking, which of course she knew quite well.

She was helping them to put away the records when Simon Hart said quietly from his corner—'Etta, I should like to take you to Glyndebourne. You would enjoy it so very much.'

She gave him a pop-eyed startled look. 'I should love it above everything,' she said.

'Good. That's settled then.'

Sandra looked across at him, too, and met his eyes. She had an odd, disconcerting feeling of having been weighed in a pair of invisible scales and found wanting. So he had not been completely lost in his game after all.

Only malice, it seemed, ever lit a spark in his eye, or jerked his features into his rather wicked smile. And Etta, of all people, was the one most likely to cause this sudden illumination of Simon's face, which in repose might have been carved out of a redwood tree. But to-night he was not smiling. 'Don Quixote and his Dulcinea,' thought Sandra, curling her lip.

She was saying to herself a week or two later that of course he adored Mrs. Prideaux. One had never thought of her as having charm or even a distinct personality until that morning when she was packing tulips to send to the hospital, and she said suddenly to Mr. Hart—'I always think that flowers go to a sick-bed like conspirators, to give one back one's self-respect. They seem to whisper that one's soul, at least, is one's own.'

He put his hand over hers. 'Voices of soft proclaim, and silver stir Of strings in hollow shells,' he said, with a bright bird-like look, like a robin breaking into a little stave of appreciation.

Bother! Where did that quotation come from? They had both spoken out of their parts, and hitherto Sandra had supposed poetry to be the prerogative, in that house, of herself and Lucas, who was by way of being a poet himself, and quite a good one. His private symbols were most intriguing.

Simon Hart was looking at Mrs. Prideaux as if she were a kind of Naiad. One saw suddenly that there was something very compelling about him, that his face was not after all wooden and that his eyes, which one had thought were like nothing so much as two little buttons of onyx, were in fact curiously soft and deep. What was he like? A dark, burnished 'cello over which a master-hand had just drawn a bow. The table was heaped with tulips, long, cold, pointed buds, flame-colour, pink and palest yellow. They rustled like watered silk under her shiny hands, and one could imagine from across the room their cool breath as not so much a fragrance in the nostrils as a very delicate sensation behind the breast bone. He was wearing, as it happened, a brown jacket with a grey shirt and yellow tie, and the light from the flowers seemed to be refracted in some mysterious way on his person, as if his clothes were enhancing the colour of the tulips and they lending his clothes a significance that a painter might have seized on.

Sandra had the oddest feeling of falling for a moment outside the whirligig of time into the timeless sphere that moves with ours like a shadow. The moment seemed unreal but to belong in some strange way to eternity, as if for ever and ever those two would stand in the sunlight and be to each other something too rare to put into words, too tenuous to be described in terms of ordinary human relationships. Never until this moment had she suspected the room of an ambience that could make it what it now seemed, a reflection of a room in a world outside time.

June slipped into July, and pink and white receded from the garden to give place to red and blue. One never got to know people any better at Closters. One had always thought that it was because they lived so much on the surface of things that there was nothing to know ... but now Sandra had a feeling of being shut out. It was because of the way Simon Hart and Delia Prideaux sometimes exchanged glances as if each knew what the other was thinking. One had the impression that they were their real selves only when they were alone together. Not that there was love, in the ordinary sense of the word, between them. It was something much more subtle and enduring. Heaven knew what qualities he saw in her that years of familiarity had never disclosed to oneself. And one had always considered oneself such a perceptive person, so aware of spiritual values.

She would never get through to them, thought Sandra, without some kind of explosion. It was Lucas, that quaint but responsive youth, who caused the explosion. He had his part in the plot.

It wasn't of Lucas that Sandra was thinking in the little copse on a slope above the garden, when suddenly like a candle carried down a cathedral aisle she saw his flaming head wavering in the gloom. She sat very still, hoping that the green of her dress would serve as protective colouring. But Lucas was looking for her, softly calling her name. There was something so lost and pathetic about him, his eyes searching this way and that, that at last she was constrained to answer him. With a look of intense relief, he advanced upon her.

'Thank God!' he said, sinking down on a mat of pine needles. 'I had a most urgent desire for your company. Etta is all very well. She is a worthy woman and her face intrigues me. She has that archaic smile that the early sculptors couldn't get rid of, and the pop-eyes, too. She makes me want to pluck out the heart of the mystery hidden beneath all that tallow. Yes—it's a face made by a primitive sculptor out of old candle-ends.'

'Mystery?' murmured Sandra. 'I don't find her at all mysterious; or the least interesting,' she added, stifling a yawn. She leaned back and closed her eyes.

'Ah! But that's where you're wrong. You can't get much out of Etta, I grant you—nothing but platitudes; but that's because she had such unspeakable thoughts to conceal. I daresay, if she chose, she could make sophisticated people like you and me feel like the Babes in the Wood. I have been holding out my hands for her to wind wool on the whole blessed afternoon, dipping first this one and then that.' He suited his actions to his words. 'Drinking in her face all the time and thinking my thoughts. And then, as I say, I had a most urgent longing for your exquisite presence. I simply had to get away and find you. You see, I dreamt of you all last night. Sandra, I dreamt . . .'

'My goodness—what?' asked Sandra, faintly alarmed. He had come so close to her that she could almost feel his breath on her face. She sat up hurriedly and found herself looking into the two blue flames that were his eyes. His long pale eyelashes flickered above her cheek.

'Sandra,' he said, in a shrill, excited voice. 'I kissed you in my dream, and I'm damn well going to make it come true.' His fingers wound themselves about her face.

'Don't be silly,' she managed to bring out, calmly. 'Let me go, please. I don't like it.'

But he held her in his long thin arms, and she had to submit to his moist young kisses and the thumping of his heart against her breast.

'This is not only unpleasant, but ridiculous,' she thought, struggling to free herself.

He let her go at last, and to her dismay flung himself down and burst into tears.

'I am a beast, and you'll hate me. But, oh! Sandra, you had no right to say I was an orchis pretending to be human.'

'Don't cry, Lucas . . . don't, my dear. I had no right whatever to say such a thing, and I'm sorry. But you don't care about me, you know. I am years older than . . .'

'What does that matter? It's part of your fascination for me, your sophistication, your experience. You know about life,' said Lucas, sadly, clasping his hands about his knees.

'Life,' said Sandra, looking mysterious, 'can break your heart.' She smoothed her eyebrows and did something to her hair that made it fall back into its burnished sweep.

Lucas sat hunched up, watching her.

'What it must be like to have the right to brush your hair!' he said, wistfully, in his reedy voice.

'Listen. The last thing I expected when I came into this wood was to take part in a love scene. I came here for peace and quiet, and to sort out my thoughts.'

'Your thoughts? I bet,' said Lucas, with a sudden flash in his pale eyes, 'they were about Simon Stink. You mayn't know it, but he's beginning to have some sort of power over you.'

'What on earth do you mean?' asked Sandra, with a look of apprehension.

'Oh! I notice things, you know. At first he was no more to you than a chair or a table or the grandfather clock. You never listened to a thing he said. It was Etta who swooped on every word and hid it in her secret nest. She's a regular old squirrel where he's concerned. But lately there's been a tenseness in the atmosphere. You come into a room and if he's not in it, your face goes kind of slack. You sit with your ears pricked, listening for his footsteps on the stairs. And when he comes in, it's as good as two glasses of sherry.'

'Really, you are being absurd!' said Sandra, vigorously brushing pine-needles from her skirt.

'It isn't that I'm jealous of Hart. I don't think you even like him. One doesn't like people who don't appreciate one. But he puzzles and intrigues you. You wonder all the time what's behind that mask of his. I do myself. I feel quite nervous when he's about. He might think me a kind of tiger-lily, for all I know. I do hope not.'

'How tired I am of this boy!' thought Sandra. She made her escape.

Mrs. Prideaux was writing letters at her bureau. Simon, lost in the depths of an armchair, was deep in a book. He rose half-heartedly when Sandra came in and sank back when she took up the morning paper.

'In a way, it's nice to be ignored,' thought Sandra, 'so calm and peaceful.'

Mrs. Prideaux lit a candle and sealed her letter. The acrid, pleasing smell of melting wax mingled with the flower scents. One can tell people's age by their handwriting. Mrs. Prideaux wrote like one's aunts. If she were writing to an intimate friend, she made great use of initials, and the word 'nice' occurred frequently.

And then the door opened, and Etta appeared on the threshold.

'Tallow—but the wax is melting!' thought Sandra. Etta's face seemed to be disintegrating under the stress of some horrible emotion.

With a vague feeling of alarm, Sandra half-rose from her chair. Simon was so withdrawn that he had not heard the door open, and for once Etta was unaware of his presence.

'You needn't go,' said Etta, pointing a finger. 'What I have to say, I shall say to your face. Delia, you've got to know. I saw her and that boy locked in each other's arms . . . in the wood. A few minutes ago. I've never seen anything more abandoned, more disgusting. One has heard of women who seduce boys, but one didn't think to meet one in your house. A mere child, the son of your greatest friend . . .'

Mrs. Prideaux had risen from her chair. She stood there, very cold and shaken, as if her favourite word had exploded

like a bomb, wrecking the surface of things and exposing something very ugly underneath. Her hand went to her heart. Mrs.
Prideaux's heart was like a shell, a delicate, hollow heart that
informed her whole being with a silvery lustre, so that the glaze
on her skin and the coolness of her voice seemed to be manifesta-
tions of something nacreous in her innermost self. Her heart had
been jarred in her breast. Her lips were blue, and a faint stain had
appeared on her neck. When moved to anger, she never blushed
as others do, but her blood made this fantastic map, as though in
violet ink, on her throat.

'Delia—it isn't true!' Sandra called out to her, imploringly.
(Oh! what had they done to her little fastidious self in this horrible house.)

'Faugh! I saw her with my own eyes. It wasn't a pleasant sight.
I was on my way to the Vicarage. I couldn't go. I felt so sick, I had
to come in.'

It was then that Simon rose from his chair. Etta's jaw dropped.

'You needn't look at me like that, Simon . . . as if I was dirt.'

'Poor little Lucas lost his head and kissed Miss Pellew. I don't
blame him,' said Simon, with a glint in his eyes. 'He is a man,
after all . . . neither a boy nor a child. About Romeo's age, I should
say. But you wouldn't know about the poetry of young love, I'm
afraid. And you certainly know nothing of Miss Pellew. If I were
to take you in my arms and kiss you, Etta, I hope you would not
be sick—as perhaps I shall one day. Who knows?' He advanced
towards Etta with a diabolical grin, and she, with a strangled cry,
fled precipitately from the room.

'Sandra,' said Mrs. Prideaux, faintly, 'tell me the truth.'

'*I'll* tell you the truth,' said Simon. 'Miss Pellew scarcely
believes in a corporeal existence at all. She is all sensibility. When
she likes people, it is for some strange, poetical reason that has
nothing to do with their reality, and that alarms them. I am afraid
she is often let down, often hurt, poor little thing . . . always looking for something she can never find. She poses, Delia—even to
herself—as a tragedy queen. But she is as innocent as the day, my
dear. You needn't turn her out of the house.'

'What a brute you are!' said Sandra, her chin trembling. 'Don't
be angry with Lucas, Mrs. Prideaux. He's rather sweet.'

'He's a very silly boy, and so affected. I think he'd better go home,' said Mrs. Prideaux. 'You have all surprised me this afternoon. It has been most disagreeable. As for you, Simon, I think you have behaved outrageously to Etta.'

'I have virtually kissed her,' remarked Simon, complacently. 'If I were to die now, she would consider herself a kind of widow— my widow in God. It's rather wonderful to lead a full life wholly in the realms of the imagination. You needn't pity Etta.'

'I must go and see about her,' said Mrs. Prideaux, putting her hand to her head. 'She is probably packing her trunk, feeling she can't look you in the face.'

Simon opened the door for her.

'I know you are going to have me on the mat later on. I am a brute, of course,' he said.

He closed the door after her and leaned his back against it.

'Yes, a brute, and a bit of a prig, too,' said Sandra, 'sitting in judgment on us all, as if you had the gift of omniscience. But I ought to be grateful to you, I suppose. At least you didn't believe the worst of me. In your own peculiar way, you took my part.'

'At a cost,' said Simon, quietly. 'I am not exactly proud of my behaviour to Etta, and I have cut a pretty poor figure in Delia's eyes, not to mention yours.'

'Mine? What does it matter about me? A rubbishy creature, a poseuse. Oh, you've made your opinion pretty plain. I shall have an inferiority complex for life.'

'You flatter me. Who would have thought I had so much power!' he said, sardonically.

'Please, don't. I can't bear any more,' said Sandra, twisting her handkerchief. Suddenly she was aware that he had crossed the room and was standing beside her.

'And yet, you know,' he said, in a different voice, very quietly, 'I adored you the moment you came into my life, with your airs and graces, wearing your broken heart on your sleeve. Your pity and your disdain, I found them enchanting. I always shall.'

'What are you saying?' cried Sandra, her eyes wide and dark with amazement. 'It isn't possible. Oh, you queer person! I believe you are trying to be most terribly kind to me. But you needn't . . . you needn't. You know everything about me, so you must know I'm fathoms deep in love with you, though God knows why! But you don't have to care for me.'

Simon's face seemed to wrinkle up like a pool when the wind blows on it. 'Don't be humble with me, my darling. I cannot bear it,' he said. He knelt down and put his arms about her.

'I can't believe it,' said Sandra, touching his lips and eyes curiously with her fingers, as one touches a remote and haunting thing brought suddenly within one's reach.

The Chosen and the Rejected

M ISS LUCY HILLIER and Miss Florence Greg had kept up a school friendship, corresponding intermittently even through the years when emotional adventures are the chief preoccupation of young women and friendship with persons of their own sex merely a relaxation from the real business of life.

But the time came when both ladies found themselves in the predicament of having no niche in life to fill, and the thoughts of each turned naturally to the other.

Lucy wrote—'Wouldn't it be fun to share a little cottage in the country? I don't think I could live alone—one is apt to become quite peculiar with no one but oneself to think about—and you are the only person I could bear to live with. We do see eye to eye in most things, and we've never got on each other's nerves. So what about it?'

And Florence replied—'Dearest Luce, what a heavenly idea! To live in a house that was at least partly one's own, and not to have to weigh every word, would be paradise. I have become quite inhibited. One's brother is no longer one's brother when he gets him a wife, and, though I have nothing against Edwina as such, she is rather diminishing as a sister-in-law. My shadow has grown considerably less. You know what I mean? Oh! I long to live near a creek, with wet sandy wastes and sea-gulls, and grow carnations in a little sandy garden. Sand is good for them, and I've never had enough.'

The cottage was found, but not near a creek. Florence, who had a passion for water, had to make do with a little brook that ran at the bottom of the garden. Lucy was delighted that one saw nothing but fields from the window, and a wood. She looked upon it as her own private wood and promised herself many poetical hours picking primroses and feeling about Nature the way the Greeks did. The dividing line between herself and a dryad would be very thin, given solitude and the light wine of ecstasy that sometimes ran in her veins.

But the wood turned out to be one of those unrewarding thickets in which nothing grows but scrub, and the trees are lean and hairy with a repulsive growth of whiskery lichen—a beggarly, untidy, rather sodden place, with a smell of something dead in it.

The cottage was not exactly period; but there was nothing in its design to offend, and, colour-washed pale yellow and with a blue front door, it was really most attractive. Anyone coming up the path could tell the kind of people who lived there by a glimpse through the window of beech boughs in a pottery jug, a copper warming-pan on the wall and little clay animals from Pompeii on the sill. There was also a witch bell which reflected a small enchanted garden on one side and on the other a mysterious white room, with two strange foreshortened ladies leading rapt and interesting lives in some remote world of dream.

Lucy was one of those women who do not photograph well because their attraction is chiefly in their colouring; but her intelligence came through always. Her eyes looked piercingly out of the pasteboard, her wild, light eyes; and people said—'So that is Miss Hillier. What an intelligent face!' She had those apple-green eyes, a pale clear skin and reddish hair, and was so thin through that she gave the impression of being as hollow as a shell. But not unpleasingly thin, only intriguingly so in the right places, like elegant antique pottery.

Florence Greg had a dark, merry face, and was inclined to plumpness. Her olive cheeks were faintly stained with pink and her mouth was beautifully shaped and as bright as rowanberries. Her dark hair had a strand of grey in it just over her forehead. Perhaps she was not quite as intellectual as one might have wished, but she had an intelligence of the heart that made her a restful companion. When she went away for a few days, Lucy missed her as one misses a fire on a chilly day.

There was not much society of the kind to which they were accustomed in the village. The vicar's wife said that the people in the great house were very exclusive and not Christians. They lived unto themselves.

'All that,' she said, 'is coming to an end. Two people living in an enormous house with a staff of servants to wait on them and more hothouse fruit than they know what to do with—it's all wrong! Arthur says if England goes Bolshie, it will be the fault of people like the Prydes.'

'It's a beautiful house,' said Lucy. 'I must say I think it would be a pity to turn it into a hostel, or whatever it is they are going to do with the stately homes. Something very gracious will perish, I'm afraid, when the aristocratic tradition is thrown on the bonfire. It is grace,' she said, 'that is so sadly lacking in those who are about to inherit the earth.'

'And whose fault is that?' asked Mrs. Smithers, rather fiercely.

'I don't know,' Miss Hillier replied, with her maddeningly tranquil air; 'but surely not the fault of those who have cared for beauty.' Her eyes looked through Mrs. Smithers, like the eyes of a leopard, at something wild and far away.

Helensgrove was a square stone house mellowed by time to the colour of old pearls. Fluted pillars supported the upper structure, and stone goddesses, mossy and bird-stained, clutched their draperies or bent their bows at intervals along the terrace.

Seen from the road, riding the green waves of parkland like a great ship, the house seemed as mysterious and self-contained as a ship far out at sea. No life could be discerned in it. No one walked on the terrace, or looked out of a window. No gardener trimmed a yew hedge. No visitor mounted the curving flight of steps to the portals. To Lucy and Florence, hurrying by, the imposing façade seemed to hide a way of life as remote from theirs as the trancelike state of the inhabitants of the palace of the Sleeping Beauty.

They were considerably surprised one day when a car drove up to the gate of the cottage, and a tall, delicate-looking woman descended.

'Mrs. Pryde!' they said, simultaneously; though neither had seen the lady before. Something of her personality must have got through to them from the somewhat unilluminating remarks of Mrs. Smithers.

'You go, Floss!' said Miss Hillier, hastily re-lighting the spirit-kettle. They must, unconsciously, have been influenced by the attitude of the village toward the exclusive lady of the manor, for they felt a little flustered. While Florence went to the door, Lucy gave an anxious glance about the room. The Cézanne colour-print and the Kelim rugs reassured her.

Mrs. Pryde stood in the doorway, obscuring Florence, and looked in with an expectant air. She had the delicate, sharp face of a fairy, with long pointed eyes, high cheekbones and a pointed mouth, like a sweet almond, above a determined square chin that contradicted her other features. 'Out of strength cometh forth sweetness,' one thought. Or should one have been on one's guard against a jaw that seemed to tether her fly-away features to the symbol of a formidable will?

She had the air of a lady who lets fashion go hang if it clash with her personality, and who sees no reason not to be pictur-esque in the country. A silver scarf was wound round her hair and a puce-coloured cape swung from her shoulders. This mauve and silver look made one think of October flowers with dewy cobwebs on them.

All this Lucy took in with her quicksilver wits before she released the long transparent hand held out to her. As Mrs. Pryde raised her hand to loosen her cape, one's eye was caught by the glitter of enormous diamonds, which seemed to heliograph the intimation that she was a greatly cherished person, and to attract and hold all the light in the room. Florence's hands looked very brown and square and unwanted in contrast.

Mrs. Pryde said—'It is so exciting that you have come to live in our little village. We are so hidden in this fold of the hills that people seldom find us out; and sometimes one longs for a little talk with one's own kind.'

'How delightful,' said Florence, 'that you should be sure we *are* your own kind! I do hope you will not be disappointed.'

Lucy could have wished that Florence were not quite so ingenuous. One should not seize on a delicate implication and put a pin through it.

'Oh, but doesn't one always know?' said Mrs. Pryde, resting her hollow cheek on her hand, as if she were about to ponder deeply upon some intricate matter. 'I passed you in the car on the Carnock road, and I thought at once—"Those are our kind of women." My chauffeur said—"They are the ladies who have taken Martin's Cottage." '

'I wonder what it could have been about us,' said Florence, carrying her a cup of tea.

'I went home and told my husband. He asked me to describe you, and I said—"One of them is like a fox, and the other like a partridge . . . only the partridge is larger than the fox. The wind was blowing through their hair, and they wore amusing clothes," I said, "and were carrying berries and boughs." '

'Now, isn't that strange! Lucy has a photograph of herself as a baby, and it's very like a fox-cub,' said Florence, looking at Mrs. Pryde as if she were some kind of sibyl; 'and, of course, I am brown and dumpy.'

'You have the soft colouring of the landscape . . . as if you partook of its nature.' Mrs. Pryde made a movement with her left hand, as if she were stroking some feathered thing. 'But Miss . . . Hillier, isn't it? . . . surprises one like a fox in a glade. I mean, one can't see a fox, can one? without a little shock of delight. And I—Christopher always says so—am like an alien figure painted on, a Regency woman who doesn't really belong.'

'How very interesting!' said Lucy, eagerly. 'That's exactly the impression I had of you.'

'Really? Christopher would love you! We seldom meet anyone nowadays who talks our language. Will you come and dine with us tomorrow? We will send the car for you.'

'We'd love to,' said Lucy. 'I think it's delightful the way we've plunged into personalities on our first encounter. One could know people for years without being told one was like a fox.'

'But personalities are so important, aren't they? I mean, they are chiefly what one becomes involved in—whether one will or no. They are the mental atmosphere of our lives,' said Mrs. Pryde, somewhat cryptically. 'I am using the word in a different sense, I know, but what is history but the play of personalities on the life of their time. The late eighteenth and the early nineteenth century is my favourite period. All those entrancing women who knew that personal relationships are the thing, cost what they may.'

The conversation that followed was delightful to Lucy, and

when at last Mrs. Pryde drew on her gloves, quenching the glitter of her diamonds, it was as if the evening star had set too soon. They saw her down the path and bestowed in her car with tender solicitude by the chauffeur. A faint scent of heliotrope still lingered in the room when they returned to it.

The car came for them the next evening and they drove through the soft landscape like two queens.

'I wonder what *he* is like,' said Lucy, in an undertone.

'People's husbands are often disappointing. They lurk in the study until one has gone,' said Florence; 'or, if they do like one, it is at second hand.'

As they approached the house, which hitherto they had seen only from afar, their pulses fluttered a little. It seemed to be watching for them with a hundred golden eyes, and the headlights, picking up the façade, gave it an even more dreamlike quality than it had at a distance. They were shown into a room so large that Mrs. Pryde at the far end seemed too little for its vastness; until she came forward like the informing spirit of so much space, and one saw that space as well as light was her prerogative. Without the scarf, her hair was revealed as of that silky mole-colour that has a greenish tinge in it like the bark of a beech, and this greenish light seemed to be faintly reflected in the ivory of her skin.

'If one were a modern painter,' Lucy thought, 'one would give her a green face.' But Florence's thoughts were on other lines; not so much thoughts, as a comprehensive flash of intuition, for which she did not attempt to find words, that for all her inconsequent chatter, the world was Mrs. Pryde's oyster and everything in it reflected in her consciousness.

'Much have I travelled in the realms of gold.' The words came into Florence's head, as she followed her hostess to the enormous wood fire that crackled on the hearth.

The door opened and Mr. Pryde came in quietly. Lucy's heart gave a little jump like a fish. Mrs. Pryde had said that he would love her; but a man with a face like this was not to be disposed of in friendship by his wife. *He won't take us at her valuation. If we bore him, he will go into his study, as Florence said, and close the door against us. We shall be 'those women' when we intrude, and less than the dust at other times.*

He had a haggard, Rembrandt face, with the deep-set eyes of a tired old monkey. It sprang out at one as if from an ambush. There was no gainsaying the voice in one's mind that told one instantly and with appalling clarity that one was caught in a trap.

'But I am not that kind of woman,' said Lucy to herself, clenching her hands in her lap. 'I have never been at the mercy of my senses. Cynical and cold, that's what I am. Look how thankful I've been, looking back, that something has always happened to prevent my marrying. Like Daphne changing into a laurel. Not, my goodness me, that any of them was an Apollo. This elderly faun—it's ridiculous.'

But she knew in her nerves that the most dangerous appeal is to the imagination. His face seemed familiar to her in some unreal way, as if she had imagined it to fit some character in a book. She could live deeply in a book. There was always the book as the author wrote it and the book as re-created by Lucy. But she couldn't recall the character to which she had given Mr. Pryde's face.

'These girls have been so clever with Martin's Cottage, Christopher. They have made it look like some dear little studio in Chelsea—yellow and blue, you know. You must really come and see it.'

'Oh, but she shouldn't! One had to make do with makeshifts; paint and pottery and colour-prints. But here, in this vast room, every bibelot was a museum-piece, and the one picture, mellow with golden light, certainly School of Giorgione, if not by the master himself.'

'He is such a hermit,' went on Mrs. Pryde. 'Wild horses won't drag him away from Helensgrove. And yet we have been such great travellers. We have been simply everywhere, even to Tibet.'

'And come back at last, having discovered that the mind is its own place. One takes one's world with one. Do you agree?' He turned suddenly and looked rather fiercely into Lucy's eyes.

'Yes, oh! yes,' she said, ardently, offering up her face like a little pale platter with a glowing fruit of expression on it. She felt tremendously elated.

'Let me take your glass.' He went to the tray and poured her out some more sherry.

'Oh, but one is my limit, really,' she protested.

'Is that so?' He stood before her, holding the wineglass between his finger and thumb, considering her with a queer twitching of the eyebrows. A smoky light seemed to drift across his face, as when refracted light is thrown by ripples on the leaves of a tree that grows by water. And then, compelling her gaze to meet his own, as if he were set on making her understand the significance of what he was about to do, he raised her glass deliberately to his lips.

A tremor went through Lucy. 'He confuses one's thoughts and makes one imagine absurd things,' she thought.

Mrs. Pryde's voice talking to Florence, and Florence's deep responses, seemed to come from very far away. They were like two people carrying on a conversation regardless of the music that was holding the two other occupants of the room in thrall.

Drama seemed to have invaded Lucy's life, even if it were only a drama of the imagination, staged in her own mind. There was a vacant place beside her on the sofa. Mr. Pryde would sink into it, and heaven only knew what things might be said. She felt keyed up, outside herself, capable of rising to anything.

But the damping thing was that Mr. Pryde, looking about, chose an armchair some way off, leaving her islanded in a pool of light and out of reach of the conversation between the two other women. One had the impression that he had retreated to some *château d'Espagne* to think his own thoughts and had left one with a rusty key that would unlock no door to his mind.

When they got back, the cottage seemed very small and horribly 'arty-crafty'.

'Everything looks so pseudo,' said Lucy, with a sigh. 'I'm afraid we are rather pseudo, too.'

'That's only because they are two such remarkable people,' said Florence, in her serene way. 'I think they are the most romantic couple I have ever met. I love their beautiful courtesy to each other, and the way he treats her—like a queen.'

Poking up the ashes of the fire, she looked dreamily into it. She was thinking that if one were to come in unexpectedly and find her in his arms, one would be as moved as when lovers come together in great poetic drama. But she did not confide this idea to Lucy. She guarded very jealously the poet in herself, the queer lurking vagabond who shrank from the flicker of an eyelash and fainted at a prick of irony. Though Florence never translated the whispers of this familiar, it was, nevertheless, his presence deep within her that made her so valuable a companion.

Of course Mr. Pryde never came to Martin's Cottage. He was not that kind of man. But Florence and Lucy were always being invited to Helensgrove, and, the more they saw of the Prydes the more they were fascinated by her infinite variety and his air of inscrutability.

One could discuss almost anything with *her*, except intimate matters; in that respect she was like women in Victorian novels, into whose bedrooms the reader is not invited to penetrate.

Florence knew something of Lucy's more flattering love-affairs, and Lucy was accustomed to expand sometimes to other sympathetic ears and to receive in exchange the not always discreet confidences of her married friends. But Mrs. Pryde was impervious to hints of past romance. She was deaf to those oracular utterances which solicit the enquiring word that is to unlock the closed door. She was not interested in love affairs, except those between historical personages. *Ne crede Byron.* Yes; that was touching and belonged to poetry. But it was no use trying to invest oneself with a little glory by recalling some moribund love. Something austere and fastidious in her forbade the exploitation of the former lover. One would as soon have dared to enquire into matters that she chose to keep private. Were they, for instance, romantically in love with each other?

Florence never doubted it. An ideal relationship had been revealed to her, and she felt about it as she felt about poetry.

But Lucy had a different conception of the relations between Mr. and Mrs. Pryde. Lucy, in her private mind, preferred to imagine Christopher Pryde as a prince whose exquisite princess did not satisfy some hunger of his spirit. Like a prince, she thought, he was capable of seeking consolation elsewhere. Oh! but a *spiritual* consolation; one that could be sought and found without disloyalty; something that was no more than an awareness in two minds of possibilities that could never become reality.

It was an exciting situation that suited her down to the ground.

He had drunk from her glass; he had afterwards neglected her. Neither action might have had the least significance but for that smoky drift of light across his face. It was that which had related the second action to the first and had suddenly brought peril and glory into her life. *You red-gold woman like a fox, you are dangerous to my peace of mind.*

Words should not come into one's head when one is dealing with an ineffable situation. She could dismiss them as mere folly, as not having constituted a thought, as having come from the same crazy region as the poetry one hears in dreams, which seems pregnant with significance until one awakes and finds it utter nonsense.

Sometimes he was brusque almost to the point of rudeness. One could then repudiate utterly the other half of one's double life. It had, simply, never existed.

And then, sometimes, a thing happened; and one slipped into that nebulous other world and played one's dazzling rôle. When, for instance, he said—'Miss Hillier, come into my study and I will show you a coffer that belonged to the Duke of Alva.'

She watched his hands slide back the panels of the coffer, and, making appropriate comments, she touched appreciatively the enamelled visages of saints and virgins on the lid.

'*Château d'Espagne* . . . why do those words come into my head when I think of you?' she asked.

'*Do* you think of me?' he said, turning and looking into her eyes.

She dropped her eyelids, and stood very still. There was a tense moment of silence, and then, with the ghost of a laugh, he turned the key in the coffer, went across to the door and opened it. Nothing had happened; but it was with the oddest feeling of having been kissed on the lips that she returned to the other room.

And yet she was able to feel guiltless, as if she had had 'an affair with the moon in which there was neither sin nor shame'.

She could play her dual rôle with amazing adroitness, being at one and the same time merely the friend of Mrs. Pryde who had come to tea, and the red-gold woman of her most secret imagination. She could say to Florence on the way home in matter-of-fact tones—'When he likes, Mr. Pryde can be very interesting; though sometimes he skulks in his study as if he hadn't much use for us.'

Florence stood still on the path, with the February skeletons of the trees behind her holding up the cold shell of the moon in their arms.

'Oh, but he *is* interesting! He fascinates me. Isn't it strange that those two should have found each other in this great world? It makes one believe in Fate.'

Her warm brown eyes, her rowan lips, her simplicity! How *noble* she was! How much more lovable than one's subtle self! And how much less thrilling to be Florence than to be Lucy!

'But you like *her* best, don't you?' Lucy said, looking back at the house that glimmered pale as the moon in the half-light, guarded by its ghostly goddesses and lit here and there by the amber square of an uncurtained window. 'Personally, I think she's a lamb.'

'I think she is the most outward-looking person I've ever known. She has so much self because everything is part of her.'

'Are we?' asked Lucy, curiously.

'Our essences. I don't know what mine is, except that she feels me kind of earthy, like loam. And the bright queerness of you, Luce. You remember, she saw you once as a fox ... something quick and secret and unexpected.'

Lucy gave Florence's arm a little squeeze. She was a comfortable person to have about. She could add her quota of appreciation to fortify that sense of her own personality that accompanied Lucy's thoughts like a golden phantom.

'Of course, she has a strong personality,' said Lucy, going on happily with the conversation, which would probably continue intermittently till they separated for the night—so potent was the spell cast by Helensgrove and its occupants.

The moon had changed its colour from the greenish pallor of newly-peeled wood to a silvery lustre as of windblown aconites, and was already throwing their shadows before them when they came abreast of Lucy's rejected wood. The dead leaves of the scrub oak that last the winter through made an eerie scratching sound as the wind stirred them, and a swollen brook gurgled noisily somewhere in the undergrowth.

Lucy gave a little shiver. The place seemed a symbol of desolation, and she hastened to speak again of Helensgrove, quickening her footsteps.

'Have you noticed,' she said, 'how that enormous room contracts into the space around Hildegarde?' (Yes; she was Hildegarde to them by this time.) 'One no longer notices the Giorgione or the flowers; or anything but her hands swooping about and her strange face. And then her conversation . . . one can almost *see* it, like butterfly wings, flitting from topic to topic; but never, never,' said Lucy, turning in at the gate of the cottage, with a thought at the back of her mind, that it was very small and dark and lonely . . . an outpost of civilization, as it were, and terribly near the fringes of desolation, with an ear cocked to hear the dreadful whispering of dead leaves and idiot water . . . 'but never, never,' she said, waiting for Florence to unlock the door, 'giving away what one most wants to know.'

They slipped inside and quickly closed the door. The faintly stuffy, warm, comforting smell of their own little refuge greeted them—a Floss-and-Luce smell of wood-ash and sandalwood and coffee-beans. Florence put on the light and poked the banked-up fire. The curtains were already drawn, the kettle on the hob, and the cat asleep on the hearthrug.

'What *does* one most want to know?' she asked.

'What there is, really, inside all the layers of petals. Do you remember as a child pulling rosebuds to pieces to find a fairy? Do you suppose one would ever get through to the real Hildegarde?'

'I think only *he* does that,' said Florence, secure in her beautiful dream.

And then, after all, the day came when Mrs. Pryde said something so intimate that they were struck dumb with embarrassment.

She was lying on the sofa when they came in, her looks more fragile and her eyes more shadowed than usual.

'My dear, are you not well?' asked Florence, hastening to her side and putting her gently back as she attempted to rise.

'I have had one of my attacks . . . nearly my last, I think. It's my heart, you know.' She touched her breast and smiled. 'One day I shall go out like a candle. It seems it is attached by a single string, and when that snaps . . . pouf! Then one of you girls will have to marry Christopher.'

There was a moment of shocked silence.

Lucy felt suddenly naked, like a goddess on a cold hillside, afraid of mortal eyes. Florence's expression was horrified and compassionate.

Then she sank on her knees and put her arms about Hildegarde.

'Darling,' she said, with a crooning pigeon-note in her voice, 'people with hearts often live to a great old age.'

'But I shall not,' said Hildegarde, without emotion. 'Sometimes I forget about it; for months I don't give it a thought. But not just after an attack. Then I know. That is why we have been living here so quietly. We don't talk about it, Christopher and I; but I am afraid he remembers more than I do. You know,' she went on, twisting her ring round and round her finger, 'he would be lost without someone who admired him most tremendously—and I think you both do that. He *is* rather an intriguing creature, isn't he? So poetic and appealing.'

Lucy and Florence cast down their eyes and said nothing. Their sense of embarrassment was so acute that they could not look at each other. It would have been easier to look at Hildegarde, who now seemed as cold and impersonal and scintillating as an iceberg, inhuman in her detachment. (Oh! but the poet in Florence crouched in the innermost recess of her being and covered his face.)

'But vanity,' Mrs. Pryde went on, reaching out her hand to a vase of hot-house flowers and extracting a waxy, exotic spray of something nameless to them, 'vanity, you must know, is his darling sin. *He* calls it pride. "I am as proud as Lucifer." He can say that, grandiloquently.'

Her lips twitched, and she gave a little gurgle of laughter. 'So touching! But it makes him very vulnerable. My dears, you must never not pretend to think him more noble than any man, living or dead. He couldn't bear it. And more fascinating. Once, after reading Donne . . . but you probably wouldn't know . . . his erotic poetry . . .' She raised her delicate eyebrows questioningly; but the movement was lost on them, who were looking intently into their laps. 'I was idiotic enough to confess that there is a poem which makes one his mistress. I might have known that Christopher's vanity would be deeply mortified . . . even by so ghostly a rape.' She gurgled again with laughter. 'We had a scene. Oh! he is quite exciting to be married to, I can assure you.

'I said to him, only the other night—"When you are left alone, my dear, you must marry one of those dear creatures. I'll pave the way," I said. And, do you know, he looked quite alarmed. He said—"For God's sake, not—"' Here Hildegarde paused, and laughed softly, looking from one to the other.

'I am not going to tell you which name. I couldn't very well, could I? But it seems, doesn't it? that the prospect of one of you does not displease him. Dear Lucy, dear Florence,' holding out a hand to each, 'I hope that one of you will not refuse to take my place.'

They took their leave shortly afterwards. There seemed nothing to say that could decently be said.

Of Helensgrove there would never again be anything to say. The chosen one and the rejected went home in silence. For very different reasons, they sought no answer to the question—which was which?

Mrs. Egerton

'A PLEASANT house to stay in,' thought Mr. Duncan Chartres. It seemed to glow with a dark patina, as though life had polished it through many years. The austere furniture, the bits of brocade and enamelled snuff-boxes, the very dovecot in the paved court, seemed symbolic. They had a message to convey. If only, thought Mr. Duncan Chartres wistfully, he himself had struck deeper roots into life, he might have been able to receive it. This feeling of his had something to do with Mrs. Egerton herself. There seemed to be a story going on in the house which he couldn't unravel. It was tantalising, like a design in a tapestry that had been worked only in places. Perhaps he, too, was part of the pattern. One thing was certain, the figure which symbolised Mrs. Egerton was an integral part. You could see that she was the tall queen in the centre of the picture; but whether Leila Barrow's fantastic face would look out of the woof, or the cloven hoof of Mr. Prinsep print a mark on the sward, or the small, sharp visage of Virginie Toussaint peer from a turret window, you couldn't tell.

He had met Mrs. Egerton's husband moth-hunting in Switzerland and had received a casual invitation to visit him some day at a house in the Cotswolds. The name was vaguely familiar. Then he remembered that a girl he used to know had married a clergyman somewhere in those parts. It would be odd if he came across her. Odd, and perhaps a little disconcerting.

But when he arrived and found that it was like a house in a book, when he had sniffed its subtle aroma, he knew that such a meeting was unlikely. And Mrs. Egerton, the hostess, with her black hair parted in the middle and her profile that was like the curve of the young moon, how she teased you with her resemblance to something once seen and now forgotten! Her silk wrap, which was sometimes twined about her but was oftener found lying over a chair, or on the stairs, or out in the garden, seemed so instinct with her personality that it was an adventure to pick it up. Its soft, warm texture and the fragrance of lilac which clung about it, stayed in the memory long after one had restored it to her.

If Mrs. Egerton praised a book to you, you found in it new meanings and a stranger beauty than you had discovered for yourself. She had that sort of power.

He liked to watch her measuring the tea out of an elegant, polished canister inlaid with a golden shell. The blue flame under the spirit-kettle seemed to be part of a spell she was preparing. The tea tasted faintly of blackberries, or perhaps it was the little spray of bramble on the yellow cups which made you think so.

And if you said—'what delicious tea!' she never replied—'It's so much a pound. I get it at Fortnum's,' like all other hostesses.

She said—'A friend of mine sends it from China. It comes in a painted chest. And sometimes he sends a little poem about a white heron, or a lover who walks in the snow, so it ought to be nice tea.'

Whenever she said 'a friend of mine', her eyelids, which were like magnolia petals, drooped over her eyes, and you couldn't help thinking that the friend must be a rare sort of person, some- one very fastidious and difficult to know, who would tell her Chinese fairy tales.

Mr. Duncan Chartres found himself wishing he had some- thing very special to confide in her. But there was nothing at all. His few love-affairs, which had once seemed so poignant, dwindled here into mere suburban flirtations, tallow-dips in the light of the full moon. He was ashamed to remember the occa- sional heartache he still indulged in after a dream of Hester Dale. Dreams are queer. After seven years or so, a woman you scarcely give a thought to now in your waking hours will stab you to the heart with some forgotten look or gesture.

'She did care after all. Perhaps the truth is that I hurt her mor- tally,' you think. You remember her little childish wrists and that she was frightened of thunderstorms and that she once sent you a pot of heliotrope on your birthday.

But it doesn't last, you know. Morning comes, and by the time you have shaved, any sweetness in the thought of Hester Dale has evaporated. You had been angry with her for years. She used to laugh at the wrong things, and her hair was always untidy. She married a curate.

One didn't talk to a Mrs. Egerton of things like that. Only very deep and true things could be confided to those delicate ears. What was there deep and true in his life?

In the presence of the depths and subtleties of the people in this house, he felt like Rosencrantz and Guildenstern. Those girls with smooth, parted hair, who sat on the sofa and talked in low tones to Mrs. Egerton, were lovely and strange. Yes, even the plain ones achieved in that atmosphere some exotic spiritual beauty. They had an air as though poems had been laid at their feet. Numerous letters came for them with foreign postmarks. They smiled secretly at breakfast over their letters, turning over the thin, closely-written sheets with their long fingers.

Mr. Duncan Chartres had only circulars, and perhaps a letter-card from his sister at Hornsey. Life, he thought with a sigh, had passed him by.

Then he remembered the bluebells in the beech wood. He would go there and paint, and forget all about luncheon. As these people so often did, when they practised quartettes in the drawing-room. In the Chartres family, one never forgot one's meals; but here they were so absent-minded that it was some-times difficult to get enough to eat. It often happened that at one o'clock, when the gong was punctiliously sounded by a long-suffering servant, none of the house-party, except Mr. Chartres patiently attentive in the hall, his hands smelling pleasantly of scented soap, was to be found. He would wish on these occasions for some business so engrossing that the common needs of life might be forgotten.

They were writing love-letters, he supposed, or reading poetry or practising the violin, leading their darkly-glowing lives with a beautiful and passionate sincerity. Whilst he stood merely waiting and listening to the old clock measuring out second by second the span of life.

But once in the beech wood, that sense of his inability to extract the magic out of the hours left him.

He stepped very carefully into the lake of blue, found a clear space under a tree, and sat down. Shafts of sunlight fell through the green tent over his head. He looked up into that strange green heaven of light, and wished he were a bird to inhabit so majestical, so emerald, a house. A gold bee blundered out of the haze, and a thrush burst into rapture somewhere out of sight. Waves of sweetness assailed his senses. He was drowned in light and fragrance and dew. He closed his eyes and sat very still. After a while he sighed and drew out his sketch book.

Many people have painted bluebells and a few have essayed poems in praise of their beauty, but no one yet appears to have captured their peculiar grace. Mr. Chartres was scarcely aware, so exalted his mood, that he was about to perpetrate another bad water-colour sketch of a bluebell wood. He opened his paint-box and surveyed the colours. Cobalt, rose-madder, a touch of Chinese white, of cerulean blue. The hours passed like minutes. His shoes were wet with dew and last night's rain-drops slipped over the beech leaves on to his coat. A careless bird splashed his hat, and it seemed a delicate little attention.

He held out his sketch and looked at it. That beech tree on the left, with the silver ripples on its sleek grey skin, was delicious, and the group of little birches on the right provided the proper balance. Greatly daring, he proceeded to wash in the bluebells. When he looked at his watch it was half-past two. He rose and stretched himself with a feeling of great elation. But he knew the deceptive nature of pictures. They play you tricks. Look at them when the mood has passed, and you find too often that the lustre has departed. Like shells out of the deep, they lose their faery hues when the light-bestowing dews have dried. But perhaps this one, unlike all the rest, would keep the tints of ecstasy. Perhaps he might even dare to show it to Mrs. Egerton. His heart beat faster at the thought.

They were having tea on the lawn when he returned. The girl with the rather large nose whose name he found it hard to remember was teasing Leila Barrow about her vellum book. Mr. Chartres quailed at her daring. It was well known that her mysterious book was one of the subjects which must not be touched on with Miss Leila Barrow. It was tied up with a silver cord in a rather difficult knot. Sometimes one came on her writing in it in an empty room, and if one did not immediately beat a retreat, she closed it with a snap and got up and went away. But of course one soon got to know a little thing like that, and took care never to disturb her when she was alone. No one had ever found the book untied.

Mr. Chartres had heard much speculation, in Leila's absence, as to its contents, but hitherto no one had ventured so far as he was aware, to speak of it to Leila herself.

Mr. Prinsep, particularly, was very curious about it. 'Do you think,' he had asked the girl with the large nose whom they sometimes called Augusta—but her real name, as Mr. Chartres occasionally called to mind, was Miss Virginie Toussaint—'that she has ever shown it to Mrs. Egerton?'

'Everyone, sooner or later,' said Augusta, 'tells a secret to Mrs. Egerton. It's as safe as whispering it down a well.'

'Innumerable people confide in me, too,' said Mr. Prinsep. 'Would it surprise you very much if she let me see that book one day?'

'Yes,' said Augusta, mercilessly, with a swift, sideways glance at his profile; and you could tell from that look that she, too, thought he had a goatish face.

Sometimes he read his poems to them in the evenings. And Mrs. Egerton listening with her rapt look would have tears in her eyes. But Leila Barrow once said privately to Mr. Chartres afterwards—'It isn't great poetry: it comes from his head. He is clever, you know, at gathering up the fragments spilled from the hearts of real poets.'

'Some exquisite lines,' murmured Mr. Chartres, remembering Mrs. Egerton's face.

'Um-m-m. Synthetic,' said Leila, with her belittling smile. That was why he thought her vellum book must be very interesting. But he would as soon have asked to have a look at it as to have asked her for a kiss. There was something fierce and virginal and secret in her air. A man might snare Leila Barrow, but he would never really possess her. As well marry a moonbeam, thought Mr. Chartres, as a woman whose thoughts are secret and inviolate.

When, then, Augusta, in her rather harsh voice spoke of the book to Leila, Mr. Chartres looked at her in a hurried, furtive way.

But Leila was perfectly calm, even smiling a little.

She looked across at Mr. Chartres, who was waiting to be asked if he had got lost, waiting for some sign that he had been missed from the luncheon table. But none came.

'We have been talking of El Greco,' she said. But whether to turn the conversation or to bring him into it, he couldn't tell.

'It is very important,' said Augusta, 'to know people's attitude towards El Greco before establishing relations with them.'

'Tea?' asked Mrs. Egerton, with her far-away look. She handed him a cup with a little fleeting smile.

'Dear,' said Augusta, putting her head on one side and looking at Mrs. Egerton in her quizzical way, 'you do remind me of a flower we used to call Black-eyed Susan.'

'It is curious,' said Mr. Prinsep, 'the number of things Mrs. Egerton reminds people of.'

'It must be very pleasant,' Mr. Chartres interjected nervously, 'to remind people of flowers.'

He wanted them to go on talking of Mrs. Egerton. It was so illuminating to discover the effect she had on others. What did the text books say of Helen of Troy and the old men at the gates?

'Yes—or trees. The most charming people I know call trees to mind—like Leila,' said Mrs. Egerton. Her dark eyes dwelt on Leila, tenderly. 'She is a willow in springtime. There is a pale haze of loveliness about her, and some of last year's dark leaves . . . like old dreams.'

Leila sat smiling, her black lashes veiling those green eyes which were the colour of peridots. Flattery in no way embarrassed her. Mr. Chartres thought she didn't really deserve admiration so exquisite. She was too sophisticated, proud and disdainful. No one was important enough to be told her thoughts. If she said anything, she said it gingerly, off the tip of her tongue, as though she told you—'You can have that much from me'—as one throws a few scraps to a dog.

But her real thoughts were locked in her secret little heart, or maybe confided to her mysterious book.

Mr. Chartres had treasured for some days now her remark about Mr. Prinsep's poetry. He couldn't help feeling a little proud that she had said that to him about the hearts of poets.

He was feeling most happy, with his sketch book tucked under his chair, almost as if he had already gained the freedom of the proud city in which they all seemed to dwell. He, too, had forgotten a meal and gone out into the wilderness to be alone. He had found ecstasy. He had never been so happy in his life. When he came back, Mrs. Egerton had smiled at him as if she knew what celestial business he had been about. So elated was he that he dared to hope he was already of the elect company of her friends; that when he had gone, she might speak of him, too, as 'a friend of mine', and droop her eyelids.

Presently they all drifted away, and left him alone with her. It was the moment for which he had been waiting. He stooped and felt under his chair.

'Mrs. Egerton,' he began. But she was strumming a little tune on the table with her fingers. 'That phrase,' she said, 'how it haunts me.'

He was rather red in the face from stooping, as he leaned towards her and said in a confidential way—'Mrs. Egerton, I'd like to show you . . .'

'Excuse me—one moment . . . I *must* catch Burgess about those bulbs.' She got up and trailed away across the lawn, leaving her wrap on the grass.

Mr. Chartres sat quite still. His heart slowed down to a quieter beat and he felt exaltation ebbing from him, as colours fade from the sunset.

If only she had been a little less absent-minded, he would have shown her his picture. He would have said . . . oh, things he had never told a mortal soul. (Surely he would have been inspired to find them to tell.)

He turned over the pages of his book and looked at his sketch.

It brought back with a rush those blue and green hours in the wood. How people got between you and your felicity! Only one person, he thought, and for some obscure reason tears sprang to his eyes, one person alone had had the gift of effacing herself behind beauty. Hester Dale. Perhaps real happiness is only to be found with the people you are not afraid of, people as colourless as water—water which reflects nothing but beauty? Only Hester, lost Hester, could have entered that quiet shrine without disturbing a leaf.

And he knew then that his picture was not for Mrs. Egerton's dark, abstracted gaze; for none of the bright alien eyes in this house.

He imagined Hester in a dress she used to wear long ago—a white dress with blue squares. He showed her the picture. 'What do you think of it?' he asked her, carelessly. (It didn't matter, really, what she thought.)

'Oh, Duncan, I *like* it!' she said, with her nervous little laugh, putting up her small freckled hand to her untidy hair. And the pupils of her eyes dilated as she looked at the picture, so that they grew dark and strange. No one had such betraying eyes as Hester, with the queerest capacity for growing from light to dark.

In his imagination, Hester's eyes grew into pools of darkness, and her nostrils twitched delicately (strange, how one remembers the odd little tricks of a woman after years and years), as she put her head on one side and looked at the picture.

'Oh, Duncan, it's so . . . so . . . *dewy*,' she said, at length, 'and, you know, you've got that wet, silver look that sunlight has in a wood in the spring. And the bluebells . . . Oh, dear! They make one faint with bliss.'

'I knew you would understand, Hester. I wish I could see you again. But you wouldn't be happy in this house. I couldn't see you, you candid child, with those sophisticated people—Oh, they are very charming, my dear; the kind of women one reads about in books, or sees on the stage. I'd always dreamed of marrying a woman like that, but until now I never met one. I've been lonely, working in the City, living in Hornsey. No one has ever talked the same language, cared for the things I've cared about. Not you, Hester. Though you had something these others lack. Sympathy, my dear. You were really rather sweet.

'I am afraid I hurt you pretty badly. But you went off with your golden head held high. You never gave a sign, did you? Oh, that riled me! I said—"Trivial little thing, she's incapable of feeling," and gritted my teeth . . .'

At this moment, Mrs. Egerton came back over the lawn, her arm linked in a strange woman's; and that faintly-golden phantom, Hester Dale, faded away.

'Another siren,' thought Mr. Duncan Chartres. Under the curve of a wide country hat, he saw a gleam of yellow hair.

He felt tired and lonely, sitting by the deserted tea-table, and hungry too. No one wanted to see his water-colour. No one cared what he thought. Their own lives, their own thoughts, were so rich and strange, what had he to offer that could possibly interest them?

He gathered up his things and retreated into the house, walking, rather absurdly, on tip-toe.

'Who is that?' said the golden-haired woman, stopping short. 'He walks like someone I used to know.'

'Oh, a queer little fellow my husband picked up. Percival,' said Mrs. Egerton, 'makes mistakes, and I suffer for them.'

'Is his name Chartres?'

'Why, yes, I believe it is. Something of the kind,' said Mrs. Egerton. 'But I can't speak of funny little men on an evening like this.' She flung her arms wide, as if to embrace the dreaming hour.

'Such beauty,' she said, 'it's almost too much for frail humanity to bear. One craves to be—why, what else but just immortal spirit?'

The other, her face very fair and innocent under the wide curves of her country hat, smiled up at Mrs. Egerton.

'Yes,' she said, gently, 'I *know*.'

'My dear,' said Mrs. Egerton, 'you are such a rest to me. There is no one to whom I so unburden my heart.'

As she said good-bye at the gate, the visitor glanced up for a moment at the windows. But Mr. Duncan Chartres was busy packing his sketch away at the bottom of his trunk. He didn't know that just at that moment life was taking some notice of him. He didn't guess how delicately ironical it was being at his expense.

What Must Be, Shall Be

WHEN Gerard Sliepley was sent to Penorth to plant conifers in that part of the county, he was a carefree young man, who had up to that time kept clear of emotional entanglements. If he was interested in people, it was purely for their own sakes and not for anything they could contribute to his inner life or to his self-esteem; and that perhaps was the reason why he received so many confidences and was called upon to give out so much sympathy.

Penorth is an exquisite place, and he fell in love with it. He had lodgings up the hill on the west side of the river that cuts the town in two as it runs down to the sea, and the view from his windows was of steep-pitched fields making a pattern of squares and triangles above the river; and beyond them, against the horizon, was the faint blue haze of the moors, like a bank of Parma violets. But sometimes there was no haze, only a straight dark line drawn at the edge of the world. Rainbows were often flung across the valley several times a day. He had never seen so many rainbows. They would fall across a larch wood and shower it with rhinestones, or touch up a white farm and make it look like a spot-lit palace. And once he even saw a lunar rainbow. It excited him very much . . . like a word from the moon whispered behind the back of her golden lord.

Tucked away in the folds of the valleys in those parts are many old houses, each with its distinctive character. Some are inhabited by lonely old ladies like the last surviving mammoths of their lost world. By chance, Gerard was taken to one or two of these by someone who had to pay a call about hens, or cuttings, or a library book, or whatever tenuous link the antediluvian owner might have with the outside world. And somehow these old ladies, who seldom put their noses out of doors because of their arthritis, or heart, or other melancholy cause, seemed to reach out their personalities as far as the outskirts of their domains. The dense thickets of rhododendron, the camellia or two, with its cheating blossoms that wither at the tips before their prime, the ill-kept mossy drive, seemed but an extension of themselves. So that, for Gerard, the acquaintance began at the gates, and he knew before the house came into view the look of resignation it would have, waiting with shut eyelids for the day of doom.

And the old ladies waited, too, in their vast drawing-rooms, against a background of fading water-colours, with a gaiety and gallantry that touched him. They spoke with detachment of the death of others, as if death were not an event that could concern them deeply. Soon Gerard, the third person, would find them addressing themselves more and more to him. It must have been that way of his of drinking people in, of being fascinated with them. They asked him to come again, and he went—next time, alone. He went, even if it meant walking a long distance in the rain. They talked of flowers and Beethoven and Italy. He liked them very much, and they liked him. Sometimes he made their old pianos sing and shout triumphantly, for he played the *Waldstein* sonata really very well; and under the spell of music something perhaps was said that pleased him very much, some delicate and touching remark like a tune played by an old musical-box.

One day, calling on Mrs. Tremayne, he found a strange woman in the drawing-room; and for the first time he had a foreboding that he was going to be more entangled with Penorth than he had anticipated. Her face gave him a shock of surprise. He stared at her as one stares at a picture or a statue, but with the added excitement of knowing that the mind behind this beauty was aware of his delight. Her eyelids flickered a little, and she looked beyond him at the door.

'Mrs. Tremayne will be coming directly,' she said; and, rising, she opened the French window into the garden and disappeared. He realised then that she was dressed in well-cut tweeds, had her hair fashionably coiffed, and was an expensive modern young woman. But in his mind he had met her naked on the slopes of Mount Ida, clothed only in light, like a lily.

'I am afraid I have driven your other visitor away,' he said, when his friend, Mrs. Tremayne, at length appeared, leaning on her ebony stick.

'That was Chloe Wilmot, with a message from her mother. She might have waited for an answer, the hussy!'

'Chloe? But could they have known when she was a baby that she was going to be pure Greek?' said Gerard, still looking rather dazed. 'She is the nearest thing to Aphrodite I've ever seen in my life.'

'Now, don't let her break your heart,' said the old lady, patting his arm.

'Surely not! One doesn't aspire to a goddess. He laughed rather hollowly. 'One knows that if one marries at all, it will probably be some mousey girl. But who is she, Mrs. Tremayne?'

'They have a house in Penorth, but they spend most of their time abroad. I suspect that cavalry officers in pale-blue uniforms, and sallow Roman princes with scent on their handkerchiefs are more Signora Chloe's cup of tea than nice humdrum Englishmen. *Lingua toscana in bocca romana*—what a medium for fantastic compliments! And to the Latin temperament what more tantalising than the rôle of the Snow Queen! Never forget that she is the aloofest white rose on the highest bough. That is her pose; that is why she went out of the window just now.'

'I've never heard you speak so bitterly before,' said Gerard, with a hint of reproach in his voice. (Like some worldly old woman in Henry James, he thought—dear, delicate, wise old Mrs. Tremayne, who was herself like a rose, an old rose with one last frail petal fluttering in the wind.)

The next time he met Chloe Wilmot was at a garden party. Crossing the lawn in search of his hostess, he suddenly saw Chloe in the midst of a group of people, and again he felt that shock of surprise. So she really was as beautiful as all that! Turning her lovely, peaceful face from one to another, she seemed to be holding a little court. His eyes rested on her face. It was like throwing oneself down on a couch of moss and primroses and letting peace and coolness flow through one's being. But presently, through some sixth sense, he became aware that, without looking at him, she was conscious of his presence, that his intentness had dramatised her to herself, and that with the limelight of his regard thrown upon her, she was constrained to act for his benefit the role she conceived him to be seeing her in. The aloofest white rose, Mrs. Tremayne had said. She was playing the part with the most delicate condescension, with a half-smile, a raised eyebrow, a little laugh, turning her turquoise eyes from one to another. A tenseness had come into the atmosphere, the lawn with its background of spreading cedar had become a set on the stage of life, and unheard strings were vibrating.

He turned away towards a Dutch garden that seemed to offer a retreat, and gusts of rose-fragrance pursued him, as if Chloe were sending out emanations of her personality to draw him back into the charmed circle.

In the Dutch garden, with its sad yews and faintly aromatic smell as of cedar-wood pencils, he found one of those Pym girls whom one met sometimes at parties—nondescript, dark girls, very much alike, who hung together and had an air of feeling themselves out of things. She was passing her hand over a tree cut into the shape of a peacock, stroking it, as if she liked the feel of the close shorn leaves, and he grinned at her rather shamefacedly as he stepped between two trees into that remote and shady place that seemed like a dark private apartment in some bright palace.

'Hullo! Are you taking refuge, too? Have you run away from something?'

'Have you?' she countered, lightly dusting the palms of her hands together.

'Perhaps,' said Gerard, 'I have run away from Fate.'

'It's no good doing that,' said this Miss Pym, shaking her head. 'What must be, shall be.'

'Juliet! She said that, didn't she? Like a bell tolling.'

'I've always thought that, too,' she said, with a startled look.

'*Have* you?' he said, eagerly. 'It would be interesting to compare notes about Shakespeare; but he is difficult to talk about—as difficult as music.' He sighed.

'It would have to be to someone so much in sympathy that it would be like talking to oneself,' Miss Pym said, in a low voice.

But at this point their solitude was invaded, and the brief exchange in the Dutch garden became as a record that is played but once and laid aside.

For it was Chloe Wilmot who came stepping lightly down the alley attended by her host, like a queen withdrawing with her chief minister from the glitter of the audience chamber for private converse in a closet. Miss Pym disappeared unobtrusively, with the dexterity one might have thought (only she was not that kind of girl) of a lady-in-waiting caught in forbidden dalliance. He stayed where he was, for he could not without clumsiness have made his escape.

Miss Wilmot's eyes fluttered uncertainly towards him like two blue butterflies. They seemed to hover over his face and to settle on his mouth, as if in that feature she sought a clue to the riddle of an unknown personality. He was dizzily aware that, for whatever reason, she was set on following up any clue she might light on, and he braced himself for the contact he could not avoid. She bore upon him in her white muslin like a ship in full sail, with Sir Ralph in tow, and by some social legerdemain that was too swift and dexterous to be assessed, contrived to be rid of her host and have herself confided to Gerard's keeping. 'God knows why she should take the trouble for a scallywag like me. She'll peel me skin by skin, till she finds I'm onion all through,' he thought, following apprehensively in her wake. Sir Ralph had gone off supposing that of his own volition he had invited young Shepley to show her the greenhouses. And to the greenhouses they went.

Hooded flowers with wicked little faces looked through the glass, like the fairies in a sophisticated production of *A Midsummer Night's Dream*. Inside, intoxicating gusts of fragrance greeted them.

Suddenly, among the lilies, she became enchanting. 'Oh, look!' she said, 'at the speckled drugget laid down for the bees to the golden throne.' She dipped her perfect nose into the trumpets of lilium auratum and breathed sighs of delight.

'You are more at home with flowers than people, aren't you?' he said, touched to the quick.

She opened her eyes very wide and looked at him, as if she were startled at the rapidity with which he had discovered the real Chloe.

'People,' she said, with a faint sigh, 'make such demands on one. One gets so tired of it.'

'I am sorry—so very sorry,' he murmured.

'Perhaps I am a peculiar girl. I like to belong to myself,' she said.

Later on, when he came to know her better, he found that she often made one naïve little confidences about herself. But she did not expect one to presume on this habit of hers. She could subject one to a lift of the eyebrows and a cool stare that were very disconcerting. It was not that she was averse from flattery. Oh, no! But she liked it to be conveyed in a delicate and oblique way that left her some excuse for not understanding.

She began to haunt his dreams, vague, troubled dreams in which he was always trying to break through some barrier to reach her, in which she passed him in the street averting her head, or went through a doorway and closed the door in his face. She was an enigma, a strange mixture of childishness and sophistication. One noticed her expensive clothes because one was in love with her, but she could have worn an old wrapper and looked just as beautiful. He was even a little shocked when she appeared once in sandals with her toe-nails painted. It was as if he had caught her reading a novel by Colette disguised as a book of poems, though he couldn't help looking at her lovely feet.

He had to find excuses for calling on the Wilmots, for he scarcely ever received a direct invitation from Chloe. He would bring her a book, or a new gramophone record, or a basket of fish he had caught. He lent her poetry.

'Simply divine!' she would say, returning it, with her little sigh of delight, that expressed so much more than she ever said.

And then one day, when the summer flowers had given place to the scarlets and mauves of autumn, when the fields were a pattern of squares and triangles delicately coloured by September, pewter and silver and molten gold, she stepped from her pedestal. They were sitting together on the sofa, looking at a book of engravings. A friend in Rome had sent it, she said.

'I suppose you have friends all over the world cudgelling their brains what beautiful thing they can send you,' said Gerard, in the half-voice he used to slip across oblique declarations of love.

'You know,' said Chloe, softly, turning over a page, 'you are rather touching, sometimes.'

'That is the first personal thing you have ever said to me,' said Gerard, after a palpitating silence. 'You had better be careful, or I might lose my head,' he added in carefully even tones.

'Might you? I wonder what would happen then.' She looked down at the tip of her shoe, with a faint smile on her lips.

'You must know very well,' he said, shakily, looking straight before him.

But at that moment, when the air was tense with drama, the door opened suddenly, and Mrs. Wilmot came in. He felt febrile, disintegrated, and when he opened his lips, a nonsensical remark came out.

'Rome,' he said, in a high, excited voice, 'it's no good spending three weeks. You want years and years. I mean, all those Apollos and Dianas—simply terrific.'

Chloe gave a little gurgle of laughter and closed the book composedly.

'No doubt,' said Mrs. Wilmot, raising her eyebrows. 'Won't you sit down again? Or were you just going?'

She had one of those cat-faces with small deep-set eyes that call to mind a she-leopard, and her blueish-white hair had the crispness of snow. It was wily of her to wear a green stone in each ear that intensified the green of her eyes.

'Yes, yes. I'm afraid I must,' said Gerard. He felt curiously light-headed. The floor seemed to slip away from beneath his feet and leave him treading on air. He shook hands so fervently with Mrs. Wilmot that he made her wince, and the sharp impress of her diamonds remained on his palm like the marks of little teeth.

Chloe came with him to the door. He didn't look at her as they crossed the hall, but when on the steps he turned and faced her, he saw from her expression that they were back where they had been. It was as if that dizzy moment had never been, as if it had existed only in his imagination. It was like the dream of the closed door.

'Good-bye,' she said, in her most distant voice. 'There is going to be a quite spectacular sunset.'

There was a smell of cut grass and watered earth. The red-hot pokers and dahlias in the herbaceous border shone crimson and yellow, purple and wine-red, and a maple and a cherry by the gate, catching the evening light, were like a golden and a ruby tree in a Chinese fairy-tale.

But Chloe had gone in and closed the front door. He did not like the word 'spectacular'. It was a cold, unfeeling word. The trees on the opposite hillside were on fire. A golden cow cut the sky-line, and out at sea the fishing-boats making for port were silver and their sails of gold. He felt at the same time a sense of frustration and strangely elated. It almost seemed that there was the taste of salt on his lips because he had so nearly kissed the Foam-Born.

As he descended into the little huddled town clustered about the quays on both sides of the river, the twilight breath of Penorth greeted his nostrils, a smell of sea-weed and tarred fishing-nets, of leaf-mould and the smoke of wood-fires. A girl was leaning on the bridge, looking into the water. An earring against the line of her cheek caught the light and shone like a drop of dew. He recognized that Miss Pym who had spoken to him many weeks ago of Fate. He had scarcely thought of her since, and had doubtless often passed her in the street without seeing her, for he had been very absent-minded of late.

But now he felt impelled to share the beauty of the evening with someone who seemed to be under its spell.

'Good evening!' he said, raising his hat.

She slowly turned her head, and for some reason he thought suddenly of Fanny Brawne—that perhaps she had a face like this.

'Isn't it fantastically lovely—like a dream,' he said.

'Like a dream dreamed by Keats,' said Carlotta Pym, in her husky voice.

'Good heavens! I was just thinking of him. Do you often guess people's thoughts like that?'

'Perhaps it was you who guessed mine, because I was thinking of him before I saw you. But perhaps the thoughts of passers-by coincide more often than they imagine.'

'That sounds an interesting theory. What a changed outlook one might have if one could suddenly have the gift of reading other people's minds,' said Gerard, approaching her side. He leaned his elbow on the bridge and looked down at the water. His thoughts, of course, were still with Chloe. If one were not so bemused, so obsessed, perhaps one could stand back a little and consider her dispassionately. If one could know what went on inside that little head, perhaps the spell would be broken, or one might be more terribly involved than ever.

'Someone,' he said, 'called it spectacular; the sunset, I mean. I don't call it a very apt word, do you?'

She seemed to take the word into her mind and consider it. After a pause, she said—'It's like the wrong thing said about music, when you've nearly died of bliss . . . like someone saying, "Now play the *Hungarian Rhapsody*", when you've just been listening to Bach.'

A faint sweet breath of violets stole from her, delicate and evocative. It occurred to Gerard that she was rather a dear little creature. He felt quite drawn towards her, as he might have been towards a small antique chair, or some appealing wild creature—a gazelle perhaps.

'One wouldn't,' went on Carlotta, thoughtfully, 'expect that person to share an unspoken thought, or a dream.'

'A dream?' he echoed. 'That would be a strange thing. Do you mean that you think two people can dream the same dream at the same time?'

'One likes to think so, but one can never know. Such dreams are only about the lo-ost.' (She gave the word a deep, forlorn sound, a chest note.) 'Otherwise', she added, tracing with her long thin forefinger an invisible pattern on the stones against which she leant, 'there would be no need of them.'

'You are drawing an ammonite,' said Gerard, surprised. 'That's *my* secret pattern. I always scribble ammonites in the margin when I am waiting for an idea. How strange that we should share a symbol!'

How long was it that they stayed talking on the bridge? Having a conversation with Carlotta was rather like listening to music, to new, enchanting music with elusive themes that give you the slip, or like reading Chinese poetry, that means so much more than it says. She was always hesitating on the verge of some communication and then withholding that which you were most eager to hear, as if to tell were to bestow too much of herself.

'You know,' said Gerard, 'you don't talk like a modern girl. You are like one of those quiet girls in a novel of Hardy about whom he says almost nothing, except just one revealing thing, like "her quickly-shutting eyes", and one remembers them always.'

She turned and looked at him. 'I think,' she said, 'I shall always remember your saying that. But to be on the safe side, I shall put it into a book I keep.'

'A book? Do you record all the compliments you receive? Not that I meant it as a compliment. It just struck me, that's all.'

'Only those that make me feel all cold, like an eclipse of the moon, as if I saw my shadow cast on another person's mind . . . not only compliments, but unkind remarks, too. And some-times,' she said, giving him a sideways look, 'what people say of one reveals not only the image one projects on their conscious-ness, but *themselves* I think,' she added, 'I know *you*. I think I have you now in a nutshell . . . in the hollow of my hand.' She opened her hand and looked down at her palm, as if she held in it some small and exquisite object.

'I am honoured,' he said, gravely, 'to figure in a psychological document of such importance. Do other people read your book?'

'Of course not. It would be like showing letters that are meant for oneself alone. Besides, flattery has no sweetness except for the person addressed, and malice, no bitterness. For a third person, they assume each other's qualities.'

'What a clear and precise person you can be when you choose! But you don't always choose, not by any means. You wouldn't tell me, for instance, what that minute thing was you held in your hand just now—the essential me?'

'The whole of a person can be expressed by a very small symbol,' she said in her provoking way. 'A tune or a scent can be everything. Sometimes all one has,' she added, unexpectedly, 'to make do with.'

Colour had stolen away from the earth and more and more stars appeared in the sky. Shimmering bars of light fell across the river as the houses on the quays lit up.

They said good-bye and went their separate ways. And it seemed to him that under their conversation had glittered all the time, like a drowned jewel on the bed of a brook, the thought of the kiss that had nearly been.

For a brief moment, some impulse had made Chloe his for the taking. To-morrow he would have it out with her, even if it meant the end of everything.

That night he dreamed again of Chloe. But this time she turned her head as she reached the door through which she always disappeared, and laughed back at him. He sprang forward and caught her in his arms and kissed her lips. But when he looked into her face, he saw that it wasn't Chloe after all, but Carlotta Pym. 'You cheat! Oh, you little cheat!' he said bitterly. 'I wouldn't have thought it of you.' 'But I have your heart in my hand and it is marked with my image,' said Carlotta Pym, and she showed him, lying on her palm, a cornelian heart that his mother used to wear on a black ribbon. He snatched it from her, and when he woke, his first feeling was one of sharp anger that it wasn't in his hand. So vivid had been the dream that it almost seemed as if Carlotta had that moment vanished through a hole in the impalpable wall that divides wake from dream. The very tones of her voice seemed to linger in the air.

The dream kept recurring to his thoughts all through the day, and when the time came to pay the fateful call on Chloe, he felt a great reluctance to take the risk of losing her for ever. He would cherish his wild hope a little longer, and in the meantime it would be soothing to talk a little more with someone who preferred Bach to Liszt, and to whom one could say anything that came into one's head. He would take her Schweitzer's book on Bach of which he had spoken. He turned his steps to the old house on the quay, which had a sideways view to where the Penorth river ran down to the sea.

Carlotta herself opened the door. He had never before seen her without a hat, or a scarf tied over her hair. What pretty hair she had, cut into soft ridges that fitted her head like a cap and waved up over her brow in a crest. Through an open door one could look through the width of the house into a walled garden, and the golden vista beyond the dark clutter of mahogany was as lovely as the remote, tranquil view in the background of an Old Master.

'Come in,' she said, not looking as surprised as he had expected; not, in fact, looking surprised at all. 'I was just going to get tea.' Long-necked and thin-waisted, in a dress of Venetian red, she led the way down a little flight of stairs and up another. He liked the way she walked, smoothly and soundlessly, as if her feet scarcely touched the ground, with a faintly swaying movement. He was reminded of a shot in a film of someone progressing endlessly down long corridors to the sound of music.

'Mother, this is Mr. Shepley. We have met him all the summer, you know, at garden-parties. But he hasn't always remembered. Perhaps we are not very memorable girls.'

She stood in the doorway, with that peculiar stance of hers, as of an angel in a renaissance picture whose wings have dropped him squarely on his feet but left him swaying, and waved a hand over the assembly of thin, brown women which seemed to fill the room.

He had the oddest feeling, as of being in a wood with fawns watching him from the shadows with soft unwinking stares. He approached Mrs. Pym. Her small dry hand lay as lightly in his as a pinch of dried rose-petals. The eldest Miss Pym, Barbie, the tall one, pushed forward a chair, and Maud and Katherine busied themselves clearing work-boxes and embroidery off the table.

'I have brought a book I promised to lend your daughter,' said Gerard, in explanation. Barbie picked it up and looked at the title.

'Are you sure you promised to lend it to her? She's got it in her bookshelf.'

Glances were exchanged and lids dropped momentarily over dark eyes.

'Now I come to think of it,' said Gerard, embarrassed, 'I offered to lend it, and she didn't answer.'

'Oh, well! She was probably thinking of something else,' said Barbie, with a shrug.

'I am so glad,' said Mrs. Pym, 'that Carlotta—it was Carlotta, wasn't it?—was too *distraite* to enlighten you, for now I have the pleasure of making your acquaintance. Sometimes you have passed this window and I have thought—"I would like to know that young man who looks like a poet!"'

'I am in the Forestry Commission and have made Penorth my headquarters for the time being. We are planting conifers, you know.'

'Such harsh, dark trees! They don't go with our landscape. Definitely, it's a pity,' said Maud.

'But I don't agree. One cannot have too many varieties of tree,' Mrs. Pym said. 'When the cones of a fir are young, they sit like little grey parakeets on the branches. There was a pinewood that was an enchanted place to me as a child,' she said, with the remote look of one who gazes through the window of the present into a small, gleaming landscape far back in time.

'We often wondered,' said Katherine, 'why you had come to Penorth.'

'We thought you might be an artist,' said Maud.

'That girl,' said Barbie, 'is a long time getting tea.' She took a cloth out of a drawer and shook it over the table, smoothing it out with her strong capable hands. She had turned-back thumbs, he noticed, and wore a signet ring on the third finger of her left hand. He glanced at the hands of the other girls. Katherine, too, wore a ring, but Maud's hands were bare. And suddenly he found himself wondering whether Carlotta ... It was with her right hand that she had drawn an ammonite on the stones of the bridge. He remembered the word 'lo-ost', the long-drawn deep sound of it. Oh! Carlotta, surely, was in the same boat as himself.

The door was flung open and she appeared with a tray in her hands. He fixed his eyes on her hands as she set down the tray and began to put out cups and saucers. They were brown and thin, with delicate pink nails like shells, and they were bare. He was aware of a deep, irrational sense of relief. He was in love with Chloe, oh! but terribly, irrevocably. But somehow he didn't want Carlotta to belong to anyone. He wanted to know that she would always be there, the same as she was now, like hawthorn that comes always in May.

Mrs. Pym poured the tea into the ancient Rockingham cups that were cracked in places.

'China—I hope you like it. Yes? Carlotta has guessed right then. She claims that she always knows whether a visitor would prefer China to India tea.'

'And, of course, she is seldom proved wrong,' said Maud, with her little sniff, 'because even persons of the highest rectitude are apt to be disingenuous in such matters.'

'But I do like China tea,' said Gerard. 'I like everything Chinese, especially Chinese poetry.'

He looked across at Carlotta, who had perched herself on the piano stool, cup in hand. 'You *do* like it?' he asked her.

She nodded. 'I make it up sometimes, as I walk, or dust the mantelpiece,' she said.

'Do you really, Carlotta? Do you really do that? I must write and tell Richard. He always asks about you, but always in a postscript,' Katherine said, twisting her engagement ring round on her finger.

'Is that flattering, I wonder? Should one be grateful for an afterthought?' asked Carlotta, with a pensive look.

'From somebody else's fiancé, decidedly yes!' said Barbie, in her deep voice.

'Well, then, it's sweet of Richard.' Carlotta slipped off the music-stool, and, crossing the window, the light from which caught momentarily her watery earrings, came and took a chair beside Gerard.

'I would very much like to hear some of the poetry you make up,' he said, turning sideways towards her profile and speaking in a low voice.

'You know what Richard said once? He said you were a bit of a witch,' said Katherine, with the crease in her young brow of one who has been pursuing a private train of thought.

'In a postscript?' asked Carlotta, in her honeyed, husky voice. (They are like the mother and the girls in a Russian play, like the different themes in a fugue, thought Gerard.)

He slipped his book unobtrusively under his arm when he rose to go. In the hall, looking down at Carlotta, he said—'The scent of violets will always remind me of you, even if you never think me worthy to hear your Chinese poetry, even if you never give me another thought.'

'Oh! But I shall!' she exclaimed, stirring with a fingertip the chrysanthemums on the hall table.

'Why should you? Your thoughts are fixed on someone else,' he said, deliberately.

She gave him a startled look.

'You cannot possibly know that. But I know *your* secret. Forgive me, but I know with whom you are in love,' she said, dropping her eyelids in that way they all had.

'I've never mentioned her name!' cried Gerard, taken aback. 'But we are quits, my dear, because I know the Christian name of . . . the lost one, who meets you in dreams, who mentions you only in postscripts.'

They gazed in amazement at each other.

'Hush—for God's sake!' said Carlotta, very low. He saw that she was trembling.

'I can't help knowing about you, Carlotta. We're in the same boat. No, not the same boat—because he loves you, I suppose, poor devil!'

'It's terrible,' murmured Carlotta, very pale, 'for two people's minds to be such open books to each other.'

'I wish to God,' he burst out, 'that we were not both in love with someone else—especially you. It's . . . it's absurd!'

'Especially me?' she echoed. 'But why, Mr. Shepley?'

'Mr. Shepley! After what's happened. It's like a slap in the face,' he said, reproachfully.

'But I don't know your Christian name. After all, till yesterday you hardly knew that I existed,' she protested, with the ghost of a laugh.

'Well, then, good night, Miss Pym!' he retorted, as if he had a right to be hurt by her lack of such elementary knowledge of him.

'Good night, Mr. Shepley,' she said very sweetly, in her husky voice.

She opened the front door and looked out.

'It's not a sunset like yesterday, to draw the heart out of one's breast,' she said.

Oh! why must she steal the very words that Chloe should have spoken?

'I haven't an earthly chance,' he said to himself, walking slowly along the quay. 'But even if I had, even if she came with me to the altar, I almost think it would be Carlotta Pym I'd find under the bridal veil.'

Lucinda

Today in the living-room at Paigles they were sitting about in their different characteristic postures.

One could not avoid the thought that the repetition of a family face induces a kind of dislike, like a hackneyed tune. Individually, they are charming, these Quarles. But, collectively, the little eyes set too close together, the long nose with the slight twist to the left, the dome-shaped forehead, grow overwhelming. One looks away with relief to the mother, whose chiselled good looks make her seem as a statue of Phidias might against a background of Hapsburg portraits.

With her blue eyes and yellow hair, Mrs. Quarles is so gaily tinted that it is hard to believe her bright blood flows in the veins of the long-visaged, sallow children whose heads were bent so absorbedly to-night over their various tasks.

They make a stranger in their midst feel lonely. They would never love you for yourself, but for some mystical reason which has nothing to do with your reality.

However, they let me come and go, sit in their midst and drink them in. And there is no thought I have not learned to read on their solemn Spanish faces. Years ago an ancestor brought back a wife from Spain. Her portrait hangs over the fireplace in the room in which we were forgathered to-night, a sombre brooding woman with tragedy in her eyes. She left an impress on that English stock from which it has not yet recovered.

I think I know them better than they know each other. A guest has not much to do in this ancient house except to poke and pry, to live vicariously in the intense and narrow minds about her. They do not dream how closely I watch them.

Venetia, aloof in a corner, was writing in her manuscript book. To it she confides her strange, troubled thoughts about God and beauty. They are written in a swift, passionate, illegible script.

To-day she had been moved by the texture, shapes, and colour of some tulips which came from London packed in a wooden box. She had extracted the tin-tacks and parted the tissue paper as though performing some sacrificial rite. (Her fingers are so long, she could almost pick a black bud on Yggdrasil or hook a Pleiad from the sky. Regal, creative hands, which seem to have a separate life, apart from her.)

I watched her take out the cold sheaves which sighed in their sleep, and touch a waxen cup with her cheek.

'Oh, Theodora!' she breathed, 'there should be some strange, jewelled adjective for this chill translucency—as though light and water were drying into silk.'

Theodora, whose fingers are not so long, almost closed her small eyes with amusement.

'Mamma would say, "Venetia is too fantastic for common people who eat mutton and puddings. She should nibble fungus and sleep in a cathedral pew." '

Venetia was silent. She loves poetry as a gardener loves the dark, wistful violets which take the airs of March with fragrance. I watched her arranging the pale flames of the flowers in jars which she set sacrificially about the room, absorbing through her finger-tips, her nose and eyes, the little, cool souls, as of Naiads, that dwell in tulips.

And in the evening, when the lamps were lit and the family gathered about the hearth, Venetia sought for the adjective Shakespeare would have used. Theodora was writing to a schoolfriend; Clare, with horn-rimmed spectacles on her prominent nose, was reading history; Duncan transposing a song into a different key; and Lewis—but Lewis was smoking a pipe in idleness, his thoughts busy with something that withdrew him entirely from the scene.

Mrs. Quarles alone looked as if she were quite aware of her surroundings. Yes, she was aware of the white walls and the old oak and the lamplight, and of the wood fire burning with a blue flame, as she turned over the contents of her workbox, a faint frown between her eyes.

'Drat that Lucinda!' she remarked presently, in her sweet, light soprano. 'The minx must have hidden my thimble.'

Her words had the effect of a handful of pebbles thrown in at a window. All the other occupants of the room (save one) started out of their absorption and looked at her with hostile eyes. I could not help signalling to her from my corner my secret amusement.

Five shocked voices murmured 'Mamma!' on different notes of the scale.

The lady's nostrils twitched with inward laughter as she looked round at the family face.

'Oh, you Quarles, with your long noses! I beg all your pardons, I'm sure,' she giggled, looking radiant, delicate and impish.

'We are your children, too, Mamma,' remarked Duncan in a gentle, reproachful voice, as he stooped his nose again over his task.

'Yes, but I've always looked upon you more as begotten than conceived, if you know what I mean,' she replied, pressing a handkerchief to her lips. 'You must forgive me for not being born a Quarles. After thirty years of marriage, I've not been able to arrive at the proper frame of mind as regards Lucinda. But you children respected her in the cradle; psychic brats from birth, Quarles, every one of you to the marrow. I *should* have liked *one* neat, pretty child, with no nonsense about it,' she added plaintively.

'Darling, there's no nonsense about *me*,' beamed Clare.

'Yes, there is, there's Lucinda. You're all possessed. You all hope, in the daylight, to catch her one day at her tricks, and you're all afraid at night that perhaps you will. Besides, Clare, there's your *face*. Papa is going down to posterity all right, but what about *me*?'

'I shall take a negress to my bosom. That might alter the strain,' chuckled Lewis from the deeps of the arm-chair by the fire.

'My dear, it wasn't a *black* woman you were thinking of when I roused you just now from your reverie. I dare say Lewis, we should all be a little surprised if your thoughts suddenly took visible shape.'

'Clare's face, and my evil mind; now what have you got up your sleeve for Theodora, Mamma; and Duncan; and Venetia? Come now, why should they be let off?'

'I suspect that anything unpleasant there is to say about the family is being said by Theodora in her interminable letter, and wittily said, too. I am not going to be baited by you, Lewis. Besides, I am only spiteful impromptu.'

'My wit,' said Theodora, outwardly unperturbed, 'is certainly sardonic. I find infinite material in the family circle, and a perfect audience in Mary Sandberg. She has a subtle, if rather cruel, humour.'

'I have no doubt that the only person you do not lampoon is Lucinda. Your own mother could not expect to be spared. I have always thought loyalty the most beautiful of the virtues,' she sighed.

'Now, Mamma, you know Theodora was only laughing at you,' said Clare. 'Of course, all this Lucinda business must be very tiresome for you; but you must admit she adds a zest to life. What Paigles would be without her, I don't know.'

Suddenly Venetia looked up with dark troubled eyes.

'I know that she is here, in the room. She looked over my shoulder——'

'Your secrets are not secure from Lucinda, my dear. There is one in this house who reads your cryptic heart,' said Duncan in a low voice to his favourite sister.

A look with which I was familiar had come into their eyes. How shall I describe it? Expectancy was in it, and awe, and a deep excitement. It is the look that music-lovers have who wait for the first strains of a symphony.

Only the bright eyes of the mother were clear and untroubled as her gaze went from one face to another of her strange children.

'She is all things to all men,' she said, and her little malicious smile flickered out as fast as a lizard that slips into a crack. 'It is time someone in this house spoke the truth about this phantom.'

'Mamma! Mamma!' cried Clare imploringly.

One found it in one's heart to pity her. I know what Lucinda means to Clare, who loves with passion the old black-and-white house with its twisted chimneys. Paigles without Lucinda would be as shallow as a roseless June. She is the uncapturable essence of the past. Sometimes one almost sees her shadow on the wall.

Sometimes, looking into a mirror, one almost surprises a face not one's own, a submerged, lost face, like a star in a pool.

'Yes, Clare,' said the light, merciless voice, 'it is high time someone spoke out. Lucinda is only a fancy name for the madness with which you are all tainted. She was invented by Robert Herrick to explain the *malaise* he suffered, poor creature, during his visit here. In his pretty way, he gave a name to the Quarles kink.'

Strangely enough, Theodora had just quoted in her letter to Mary Sandberg an extract from her ancestor's memoirs:

> '*Bob Herrick from Dean Prior to stay a sennight. I would for my part it were twice as long. His conceits much after mine own heart. Will have it that a spirit walks at Paigles—one who gathers the invisible roses of the Moon. Eye hath not seen but heart hath felt her quaint enchantment. Aye, a poet's heart. I would not that Luisa, my wife, had wind of this most incorporeal Beauty.*'

Looking up, Theodora repeated the last words, her small eyes glittering.

'Mamma, being a beauty herself, can't do with this incorporeal rival,' said Lewis.

Mrs. Quarles' nostrils twitched again. 'If it weren't for my Attic sense of humour, I should surely perish of a sense of my own unworthiness,' she said.

She now heaped up her bright wools in a basket and, still holding in her laughter, went out of the room.

'What did she mean?' asked Venetia, a worried pleat between her brows.

'I suppose we rather make her feel there is something special about us—this Lucinda ichor in our veins which sets us apart from common humanity,' said Theodora, folding up her letter. She lighted a candle which stood at her elbow and held in the flame a stick of sealing-wax.

The others watched her deft fingers at work with eyes which looked fascinated, but were in reality dark with abstraction. Finally, she set her seal upon the yielding wax and watched it set into a crisp device with a pleasant sense of secrecy.

But she didn't feel quite so secret as usual. Her mother's remark had disconcerted her. Mamma was diabolically acute. But the others hadn't noticed it.

After all, was she not conferring a kind of immortality upon her family, making them come alive for Mary Sandberg in the realm of Art? For she drew them a little more grotesque and fantastic than life, as though her mind turned a limelight upon them. She made them dance to her secret tunes, like a malicious showman dangling his puppets.

'It must exasperate her to distraction. Why, she doesn't even *believe*,' said Clare.

'Beautiful as she is, she is nevertheless material to her finger-tips. Those sweet, as she would say *tidy* little faces, have faith only in what they can see,' said Theodora. 'I adore Mamma, she has such a caustic wit—but as for anything else ... She walks with light feet over wells of darkness, never hearing the stones ring hollow.'

'I sometimes think,' sighed Venetia, slipping her book behind a cushion, 'that if it were not for her, we, some of us that is, would *see* Lucinda.' She exchanged a look with Duncan. 'Sometimes she seems so close. She was just now. But Mamma with her commonsense is like—is like—electric light in a room which a moonbeam is trying to enter.'

She pushed up her heavy hair with her long hands as though it were a crown she would fain lift from a brow grown weary. 'Duncan in his music, I in my poetry—sometimes she almost gets through to us.'

Theodora giggled. She had written to Mary Sandberg, 'Mamma says "Duncan's music is like an orgy of grasshoppers." Not a bad description for this scratchy modern stuff, all broken reeds and frustrated rhythms.'

'I sometimes think,' said Lewis, 'that we are all as mad as hatters, and that Mamma, with her scepticism and her common-sense, must hate the stink of occultism there is about this house.'

'Stink is too strong a word for the delicate perfume of Lucinda. What is she to you, Venetia?'

'Poetry,' said Venetia.

'Music,' said Duncan.

'I suppose, history—the sense of the past,' said Clare, slowly.

'With her help, I turn life into drama,' said Theodora.

'Since Theodora has dragged us all into the confessional and has herself confessed,' said Lewis, 'I suppose I must add my dark secret. Lucinda, to me, is just—woman. I have committed adultery with her in my heart.'

Upstairs in her bedroom, Mrs. Quarles was writing in her diary:—

'Abused Lucinda to the family; told them she doesn't exist. I hug my secret to my heart—it gives me infinite joy. Saw her again to-night in my mirror. She made a moue before she disappeared. What should we do without each other? Is it not a celestial jest that I who am no Quarles alone know her? I know her funny, malicious mind, which is akin to my own. When I make my little jokes, it is Lucinda, bless her, who laughs the deepest. I know she is rippling all through her crystal, as when you throw a stone into a pool. I alone know that she has hair the colour of amber and eyes as blue as squills. . . .'

But here I was too impatient to read any more. For my hair is raven-black and my eyes are green. She has not seen me—only her girlhood's face in the glass.

Alas, poor me! Poor lonely ghost!

The Keys of Heaven

IN A WAY, she was preparing a funeral feast for something that might have been. But the lily-of-the-valley cups, so old and delicate that really they should have been safely under glass in a museum, were not too precious for her lost friend; and she took them out of the china-cupboard with a deep, sad pleasure, touching them reverently.

Her mother's portrait looked down from the wall. She, too, had treasured the cups and had kept them for the secret festivals of the heart, in honour of a person here and there whom no one had guessed she delighted to honour. It was the portrait of a lady not so golden as her daughter Irene, and not so brown as her daughter Jane: betwixt and between with mouse-coloured hair and greenish eyes. She held a rose in her long, pointed fingers, and the artist had set a sparkle in her amethyst ring.

The same amethyst now shone on Jane's hand as it moved to and fro, between the table and the corner-cupboard. It always seemed to Jane that the pattern on the cups, the cool lily-bells and green leaves and faint lines of dark-blue, vermilion and gold, sang a tune out of the past, like a tinkling air played by an old musical-box.

A pinch of Orange Pekoe in the tea, and some lemon, perhaps? One never knew. She had no knowledge of his tastes. She knew nothing about him at all, she suddenly realized, not even a little thing like that.

He was sitting in the white, flower-scented room on the other side of the wall, with her sister Irene; and his presence seemed to burn through bricks and plaster, making a warmth in the sombre red-walled dining-room, pervading the entire house, as though it were a desert and he a solitary camp-fire. When he went, there would be ashes and silence. But no need to think of that yet. No need to think of hereafter.

The portrait on the wall looked down at the younger daughter of the house carefully rubbing up the Queen Anne teapot with a velvet cloth, at the delicate array of china on the tray, the austere mahogany furniture and the vase of chrysanthemums on the table. The original of the portrait had always thought that her daughter Jane had one or two physical attributes which even her daughter Irene might have envied: exquisite dark eyebrows so fine that they might have been printed in with Indian ink, and a long neck that gave her head the air of a harebell delicately poised on its stalk. She had witty fingers, too, with a way of touching even common things as if they were rare. She could dress up a salad so imaginatively that it seemed a pity to mix it up and eat it, and her bowls of wild flowers had the immortal, haphazard look of an Impressionist still-life. But the portrait was of a lady who had seen more than most people. She had not been too dazzled by the golden daughter to see the brown one with the clear gaze of love . . .

Lizzie, the maid-of-all-work, looked in.

'Lor, Miss Jane! We don't have those, not for the Squire and her ladyship,' she said, round-eyed.

'But the pheasant cups are very gay, too, Lizzie,' said Jane, with circumspection, 'Lady Rowland likes them.'

Apple-cheeked Lizzie was experienced in love. She had a peasant's instinct for divining its hiding-places and would sometimes confidently assert that some village lad was 'sweet on' a girl long before either party had betrayed by word or sign that such was the case. Lizzie, with her turned-up, inquisitive nose, suddenly took on the aspect of a pig snuffling after a most rare, deep-hidden root; and Jane felt cold with a kind of agony. She raised her dark eyebrows and looked so quizzically at Lizzie that the maiden retreated somewhat abashed. Miss Jane, in Lizzie's eyes, was almost ugly; but she could make one feel as if one's hands and feet were coarse and enormous. Miss Irene had given her ever such a sweet dress, almost new, when Bob Willett had thrown her over. 'There now, Lizzie,' she had said, 'you let him see how little you care!' But Miss Jane had heard her crying in the night, and had come in and sat on her bed and comforted her. So she loved Jane, while she despised and pitied her. For anyone who went to the movies at the nearest market-town on her evenings off could tell that Miss Jane had no sex-appeal. Whereas Miss Irene . . . In Lizzie's opinion Miss Irene was more beautiful and heartless than any vamp on the screen, and to be in service at the Rectory was almost as good as playing a small part in the pictures oneself . . .

And now, the mysterious dark gentleman who had lately come to the village—a bit of a foreigner he looked—was alone with her in the drawing-room. To be sure, he had asked for the Rector, who was not at home; but Miss Irene had intercepted Lizzie on her way to the door and had given instructions that he was to be admitted. Perhaps this time she had met her match . . .

The dining-room dreamed in its reddish gloom. The afternoon light spilled itself on the mahogany, making little pools of gold in the polished surfaces. It ran a fingertip along a gilt frame, and shone through the wine in the decanter, and drew sharp odours from the apples on the dish. The Hepplewhite chairs, ranged sedately against the wall, seemed lost in memories. They were remote from the present, withdrawn and delicate; like ancient great-aunts who no longer care which of the children are in love.

That's how they seemed to Jane. She was in love, and nobody cared. Nobody, thank heaven, knew. In love . . . but it was more like being possessed by the devil. The very idea that she might ever be attracted by one of Irene's young men had frightened her, the desolation of it. Irene's admirers were hard to talk to. They didn't put themselves out for mousey girls like Jane . . .

Sometimes the two sisters would be asked to dine at some neighbouring house and a car would be sent for them.

'What a bore!' Irene would say. She was clever at ringing the changes with a black frock and a white one, and somehow contrived to look as if she had several dresses.

Jane had only one evening frock, an oyster-coloured silk, with which she wore a brown coat and some amber beads. But it didn't matter. No one noticed that she wore the same dress over and over again. She was only a shadow in the wake of the white and golden beauty.

Irene was shown off by her hosts to visitors. Jane could see them doing it. She could tell by the expectant look on the faces of strangers that they had been promised a treat.

When they got home, Jane would have to take an aspirin, because her head ached and she was so tired of talking to people who made her feel as if she had been looking into empty biscuit tins and seeing only her own distorted face gazing back at her. But Irene would say, serenely unclasping the pearls about her white neck—'It was rather amusing after all, wasn't it?'

One spring morning, Irene came in quite excited from a walk to the village. 'My dear,' she said, 'I have just met the new tenant of the thatched cottage. He was buying stamps and seed-packets at the stores. I looked at him—and he looked at me, very hard indeed. Do you know what he is like? The portrait of Sir Philip Sidney you have in your room ... one of those haggard, pear-shaped faces, you know. I think,' she added, smiling, 'that he was slightly intrigued.'

Jane looked a long time that evening at her picture of Sir Philip Sidney, and thought for the thousandth time that he had the most beautiful face in history (which, of course, he has); and for some unfathomable reason her heart misgave her.

The stranger's name, they soon discovered, was Edward Revell. He wrote, or something, and had come to the village for quiet. So much they heard from Lady Rowland. And presently she added that the man had no manners. He had refused her invitations to dine, at first with conventional excuses, and then so curtly that it was clear he thought her importunate.

He seemed as content with his own company as Jane with hers.

Of course he was not really like Sir Philip Sidney, but Jane could see what Irene meant. He had the sort of sharp-set face that one can tell at a glance is terribly vulnerable to beauty. They met him sometimes in the village ... and if he looked at Irene with a complete and almost ruthless absorption, assuredly Sir Philip Sidney would have done the same. And sometimes his glance would light on Jane, as of one who might notice some little thing about Iras or Charmian, because of the glory of Egypt that shone accidentally upon them.

But it was not until September that they became acquainted with the elusive stranger.

A short week ago—and yet it seemed like a thousand years—Jane had met him up on the Downs, in the Roman Camp, and they had had so interesting a conversation that she quite forgot she was only the plain Miss Ritchie.

She went to look for a book she had left in a thymey hollow which she had long considered sacred to herself. There were tussocks of grass in it that made restful cushions for a thin body, and it was pied with blue and yellow flowers—coltsfoot and scabious and cold sea-thistles, and butterflies flew in and out again on their delicate, inconsequent affairs. She would lie there for hours and dream, watching the drifting clouds take on their fantastic metamorphoses. And when one was tired of white and blue and the way of the wind up aloft, one could turn to earth and rest one's eyes on the dove-coloured breast of the downs, dappling from fawn to grey as the cloud-shadows passed over them.

Far away, on the road the Romans made, there might be a horse and cart plodding slowly through the loneliness, or a shepherd on the sky-line. But no one near to disturb the blessed solitude.

She stood poised on the ridge and looked down at him, seated on a cushion of thyme with her book in his hands. Her shadow falling sharply across the pale grass caused him to look up. Just as she had come to the conclusion that she would retreat without a word, because he had too formidable an air for approach, his dark glance swept over her, and he rose and bowed gravely, his shadow bowing too, in a stately, Spanish sort of way, and lying very sharp and clear-cut on the grass.

'I am sorry to disturb you,' said Jane, 'but I came to look for a book I was so careless as to leave here.'

He held it up towards her.

'I meant to drop it at the Rectory on my way home,' he said, in a matter-of-fact voice, as if they were already well acquainted.

'But how did you guess where it belonged?' asked Jane, in surprise, her eyebrows going up into two thin dark arches. 'I do not think there is a name in it.'

He smiled in that dazzling mysterious way people have whose smiles are an event to their friends and make them feel elated and yet a little unworthy, as though they knew that nothing in them merited such warmth and brightness.

'I suppose that knowing him' (he tapped the book) 'to be rather a recondite ghost, I thought of the likeliest haunt, and you came at once to my mind.'

'That interests me,' said Jane, and a faint tremor of surprise seemed to flutter her a little, as if she were a harebell caught in a puff of breeze, 'especially as I cannot remember that you have ever *seen* me before—not, I mean, even so much as to notice perhaps that I have brown eyes and hair.'

'Perhaps not,' he conceded, looking away into the depths of the valley, 'details often escape me.'

After a pause during which he seemed to be considering the view—so near that it seemed as if one could scoop it up in one's hands and dip one's face into it—he turned towards her again.

'Do you know the experience of being ravished by a poem and then finding that you cannot remember a single thing about it, except perhaps that there was a star in it? And yet the poem seems to live on, complete and immortal, somewhere deep in your experience.'

'I think I know what you mean,' said Jane, doubtfully, hoping that he might return to the opening theme before developing this further fascinating, though impersonal subject (all unused as she was to be talking of herself). 'But,' she went on, conscientiously trying to answer his question, 'I have a very good memory and if I read a poem with concentration, it stays line by line in my head—like a bird in a cage, perhaps, instead of a kingfisher flashing past.'

'And people . . . do you arrive at your knowledge of them little by little, weighing their qualities in your invisible scales, until at last you have discovered the truth?' he asked, cocking his head on one side, like a listening bird, and watching her with black, glinting eyes.

'I think I do,' said Jane, smiling. 'It sounds very cold and calculating; but one doesn't often see the whole truth of a person in a flash—out of the blue.'

'Brown eyes and hair,' he said, 'I see now; but it hasn't added to my knowledge. It must have been something else that made me say—"This is her book." But you have not,' he added, turning over the pages rapidly, 'marked my favourite passage. Listen now.'

His voice was low-pitched and resonant and so in time with the music of the downs, the trilling of larks, the crying of plovers and the sound of church bells blown up from the valley, that she was reminded of the 'cello in a concerto. The words she knew very well, but spoken in that lonely place they seemed to have undertones she had not heard before, to reach beyond language into the sphere of music.

She sat down on the bank and her shadow folded itself beside her like a cloak she had dropped. But when she took off her hat and turned a little sideways to the sun, it went further away and became a dark woodcut of a woman in a reverie.

An orange butterfly, as though possessed of an instinctive sense of decoration, fanned its wings on the metallic blue of a sea-thistle close at hand, and beyond, in the valley, the view was clear and small, like an opal one might wear in a ring.

Mr. Revell finished the chapter and put the book down beside Jane. Her wandering thoughts came back, and she gave a little sigh.

'What sort of books do you write?' she asked, resuming her hat.

'After the *Religio Medici*, perhaps you would hardly call them books,' replied Mr. Revell, deprecatingly. 'I dig about the roots of ancient literatures and worry students with my discoveries. Text-books, you know.'

'I suppose,' said Jane, musingly, 'that being so very learned makes life an absorbing business.'

'Let us talk about life, let us scrutinise this mysterious thing. Shall we?' He sat down beside her on the bank.

'What do you make of it?' he asked, clasping his hands about his knees and bending towards her.

'It has everything to do with *being*,' said Jane, slowly, pondering the matter with her chin in her hand, 'and very little to do with *doing*. Some people are wrapped in it like a cloak they always wear—my mother was like that—but others seem to keep it in a drawer and take it out only when something happens to them. In between events they are not aware of life.'

'And you?' he asked.

'I wear the cloak,' she said, 'but it changes its texture. Sometimes it is all the colours of the rainbow, and sometimes—mere sackcloth.'

'Yes,' he said, stooping to pick a little flower, 'one has to pay the price of ecstasy.'

He put the little blue flower in his buttonhole, and with its fairy face and soft black eye, it almost seemed to be taking part in the conversation—so confiding and intelligent it looked, so innocent and gay.

'But isn't happiness *queer?*' said Jane. 'The way it comes—oh, just out of the air!'

And after that they talked, as it seemed afterwards, thinking it over, of everything in heaven and earth. Once, in a pause of their conversation, she had time to think—'I suppose I always knew that there must be people like this on earth to talk to.'

It was on the way home that she remembered Irene. As she went down the hill, she thought with surprise—'Irene is at this moment arranging the chrysanthemums, or making an apple-charlotte.' It almost seemed as if she had stolen a march on Irene, waylaid an adventure that was hers by right. For it had been tacitly assumed between them that the situation was a flower waiting to be picked. When the time was ripe, Irene would stretch out her hand and gather the rose of Mr. Revell's admiration.

On the threshold of a new adventure, she could be charmingly reticent. It was only afterwards, when the flower was gathered and laid in her lap, that she plucked off the petals for a friend's amusement.

'Jane,' she said once, with her little cynical laugh, 'thinks that women who talk of their love-affairs are simply awful. But that's because she never has any.'

It occurred to Jane that Irene would certainly have discovered what it was that Mr. Revell had seen which told him at once so much and so little about her—not what she looked like, but the kind of books she read. Irene wouldn't have taken it as a compliment; and perhaps it wasn't. But more interesting, surely, even than admiration.

For a few days life was radiant. There seemed a richness in the atmosphere, an incense, a fragrance, as of Roman hyacinths in the rain. Some people, Jane reflected, have a quickening power, like music. It wasn't a question of personal relationships—often they are aloof and impersonal, such people: it was a question of spiritual values. And she made the illuminating discovery that it is by what he thinks important that a man either enriches life or impoverishes it.

And then she remembered that already, perhaps, the shadow of personal relationships lay across the future; already, perhaps, he was caught in Irene's net.

'Why should it matter? He will still be himself,' argued Jane to herself.

But the situation got out of hand. It went on developing in a mysterious way. That hour on the hillside, instead of being complete and rounded-off like a one-act play, had become the first act in a never-ending drama.

Sometimes a word or two of the dream-conversations survived the night. They made nonsense in the light of day; but had a magical sound—key words to some tremendous secret. It seemed as if she and her friend had progressed so far in intimacy since their first and only encounter that they might have known each other a lifetime. She could scarcely believe that this progress was after all a one-sided affair, and that for him the experience had ended on the hillside, when she had said good-bye and walked away with her book under her arm, her long prim shadow following at her heels.

So much happened in the space of a week, and yet nothing at all happened (because she did not see Mr. Revell during that time or even hear his name) that the experience of years seemed compressed into it. He seemed to come between her and life itself, so that it seemed scarcely worth while to do anything but sit with folded hands and dream, drifting she knew not whither; but now and again she was afraid that it was to some bleak island of pain.

At the end of the week the inevitable happened. Irene came back from a dinner-party at the Hall with the news that the elusive Mr. Revell had been driven at last to accept an invitation.

'He took me in. Jane, he's an intriguing wretch,' she said, looking down at Jane's pointed face on the pillow.

By the light of the moon, Jane's eyes looked like two wet dark flowers under her winged eyebrows and the peak of dark hair that grew on her forehead. In the moonlight, her mahogany bed and the white-and-black of her pointed face on the pillow and the narrow shape of her body under the coverings had the mysterious look of an old engraving. But Irene in her silver coat seemed to catch all the refulgence of the moon. It shone in the red-gold of her hair and turned her neck to alabaster; not putting out her colours, but clouding them over with a nacreous lustre.

'You didn't tell me, Jane, how easy he is to talk to. I had imagined that he would be rather silent and formidable; very deep water to fish in,' Irene said, with her light, tinkling laugh, and walking across to the mirror, she looked at the faintly-tinted image reflected there.

'I look,' she said, 'like the ghost of Mary Queen of Scots. Tell me, Jane, what did you talk of, that time he found your book on the downs?'

'Oh, I don't know—poetry and things,' said Jane, in a flat, weary voice.

'Are you very sleepy, darling? Aren't you interested in my dark man?'

'Oh, yes. You know I told you he seemed very nice,' said Jane, turning her face to the pillow.

'You know,' Irene went on, idly unscrewing a scent bottle on the table, 'one isn't just a pretty woman in the eyes of a man like that.'

'Anyone can tell from the way he stares that he thinks you as lovely as Venus; and so, of course, you are,' said Jane.

'Mark my words,' Irene laughed softly, as she opened the door, 'he will return Father's call in a day or two.' And Jane heard her singing 'Madam, will you walk?' through the wall. She lay awake long after Irene had ceased creaking about in the next room and singing . . .

* * *

So that was why Jane lingered in the hall with her hand on the door-knob. Their voices came muffled to her ear. She saw the white room with the eye of her mind. She had filled it with the sweet, uncertain roses of September, which either open all their petals at once, passing from tight buds to a full-blown precarious grace, or else remain obstinately buttoned up and wither with their sweetness all unknown. And she knew that the light would be intensely golden, with the still quality it has in rooms which face east after the sun has gone on.

A sound of approaching footsteps—the ubiquitous Lizzie's—made her turn the handle and walk in.

Irene said—'You have met my sister, I think,' and she found herself shaking hands and meeting the gaze of his dark eyes as composedly as if Irene's remark were entirely adequate to describe the situation. As perhaps, she remembered, it might very well be so far as he was concerned.

Her first feeling was one of astonishment that he was, after all, quite a small thin man. It was like seeing an actor after a great performance without his make-up. She was almost elated to find that his eyes, which had seemed deep enough to fall into, were not so large after all. Indeed, they had almost a beady look, she told herself.

'What a dance you have led me!' she thought, smiling. And with that little mysterious smile still curving her lips, she dropped his hand.

Irene went on with the talk that had been interrupted. Her voice was apt to linger over words, pulling them out with her drawl until one thought of toffee, making them memorable and fascinating.

'I think Chopin is too divine,' she was saying. 'Jane says he is all roses and moonlight and someone creeping broken-hearted down an avenue of yews, but I *adore* his melancholy. I should like the *Ballade in A flat* to be played when I am dying. I should like the little phrase' (she hummed it, beating the air with her hand) 'to be the last sound I hear on earth. Remember, Jane!'

'My dear,' said Jane, in a bitter-sweet voice, 'you must tell your grand-daughter. I hope to be dead long before that.'

'Have you no wish, then,' asked Mr. Revell, smiling, 'to be a great-aunt? But I think, you know, that I see you as the little old lady who knows the best fairy-tales.'

'Why?' enquired Jane, surprised.

'Well,' he said, considering her with his head a little on one side, 'it seems to me that I have seen you look out of the window at the end of a Hans Andersen story. You have raised your eyebrows at me, standing out in the snow, and pulled down the blind. Wouldn't it be a pity,' he said, turning to Irene, 'to waste such ironical eyebrows?'

'Of course,' said Irene, smiling, 'and I can imagine the young ones taking her their broken hearts to patch up. She'd be kind, but caustic. She'd say—"There are as good fish in the sea!" and "where's your pride, boy?"'

'But I shouldn't need to,' said Jane, quietly, 'if they took after their grandmother.'

Irene made a little grimace, and Mr. Revell laughed, looking from one to the other under half-closed lids.

'But suppose,' thought Jane, suddenly troubled, 'she were to break his heart.'

She stole a look at him. He was leaning back in his chair, looking at Irene with his bright, dark gaze. Last night she had been smoked by the moon into mother-of-pearl, but in the mellow afternoon light she was as sparkling as a May morning.

'Talking of Chopin, I hope you will play to me some day, Miss Ritchie,' said Mr. Revell.

'I don't play to everyone,' Irene said, with her little ensnaring smile in which her eyelashes also took part fluttering an instant on her cheeks and looking so alluringly black in contrast to the tawny brightness of her hair. 'But perhaps,' she added, choosing a pink rosebud from a vase near by and fastening it into her dress, 'perhaps, one day, I'll play to you.'

'But sing to us, Irene, till tea is ready,' said Jane.

So Irene went to the piano and sang some German *lieder*—some of the love-songs of Brahms.

Jane leaned her cheek on her long thin hand.

'Love isn't the whole of life,' she thought, with a feeling of tears in her throat. 'There is all that loveliness out there—that used to be enough.'

She thought wistfully of the time when happiness came out of the air; of the High Lakes at sunset, and the little dark birds floating over the glassy deeps, the cool rushy smell, the mystery, as of water gods hiding. She remembered the winter twilights, with a shell of a moon in the east; and the thought of spring was a pain in her heart. Windflowers and yellow palm and cowslips . . . the keys of heaven. Would the spring keep for her its ancient ecstasy?

The Keys of Heaven. Once they were hers for the asking, but now it seemed that the dark man in the corner had taken them and put them in his pocket. It was queer that Irene with her passionless heart should sing so beautifully that one wanted to cry.

She turned her head to look at him, to watch him secretly whilst his being was emptied of everything but music, as hers could not be in his disturbing presence, and was startled to find herself looking into his dark shining eyes.

He looked away quickly, with such a guilty air that she knew he must have been studying her, defenceless and unaware, with her thoughts printed on her face. Goodness only knew how much those penetrating eyes had seen!

She had an odd feeling that the music had made her as clear as glass, and her cheeks were faintly flushed as she bent over the tray.

Irene swung round on the stool, and Mr. Revell thanked her in a very quiet voice that revealed his deep delight.

'It would be interesting to know if one would sing them better or much worse for being in love,' said Irene in a conversational tone. But Mr. Revell was looking at Jane with rather an abstracted expression and did not reply.

As she filled the lily-of-the-valley cups, Jane thought that no one but herself would ever hear their little tune. Mr. Revell carried Irene's cup across to her and coming back for his own startled Jane. Holding it up he said, suddenly—'What an enchanting design—like a little air by Scarlatti!'

Jane looked at him almost with panic in her brown eyes. It was a remark that did not belong to reality . . . like something he might have said in her dreams.

'Why, Jane, it's poor Mother's precious china. We have not used it for years,' said Irene, surprised. 'You know,' she went on, turning to Mr. Revell, 'you ought to be flattered that she has taken out the best china, which Mother used to keep for special little feasts.'

'Did you guess,' asked Mr. Revell, in his disconcerting way, 'that I should like it very much?'

'So few of our visitors,' murmured Jane, confused, 'ever notice anything that is lovely. I think of the time when people quoted Pope and wore red-heeled shoes and tea was called "tay". I think of them drinking out of these cups, and someone, perhaps, playing the spinet. And it makes the tea taste rather delicious,' she ended, breathlessly, looking from one to the other of her listeners with an apologetic air.

'But it is rather a prim little pattern,' Irene said. 'There is nothing in it except a few faint lines.'

Mr. Revell and Jane smiled at each other as though they shared a secret. And his smile, always like a falling star, seemed to drop through Jane's eyes into her heart.

It was Lizzie, after all, who was the first to understand. Coming in with a plate of hot scones, she nearly dropped them.

'The love-light!' said Lizzie, so thrilled that she almost said it aloud. And going back to the kitchen, she sang, out of the fulness of her gay, experienced heart, the song Miss Irene was always humming about the house. 'I will give you the keys of heaven,' sang Lizzie, with the abandonment of a thrush in springtime.

The Golden Rose

SHE lived by herself in a little house down in the village, Some-times she was asked to a tea-party of local ladies at the Manor, but never to meet any of my stepmother's friends from London. I used to feel ashamed of my father and Julia, and deeply apolo-getic towards Aunt Essie. I would hold my thumbs for her when parties were being discussed, and would pray with pop-eyed fervour, till my veins stood out, that God would make them ask Aunt Essie.

Why must my father, her own brother, take his cue from Julia? He had no *right*, I felt passionately, to consider her objectively, with the eyes of a stranger like Julia, who had come into our lives fortuitously, bringing her own world with her and blowing out the one we knew like a soap bubble. Looking back, I think it must have been that he was aware of an inner conflict, of being torn between the quick and the dead, and that he chose the easy, mas-culine way to peace of mind by repudiating the dead. Because Aunt Essie belonged to the world that was gone—my mother's— the safest thing was to forget that she had once been a light in the mind and a fragrance in the memory; and to substitute, for the delicate impressions that constitute for one a beloved personality, the slightly absurd figure that Julia saw with her black-velvet eyes.

Julia was a parrot-tulip, an elegant but gaudy creature with a variety of selves, one for each person who mattered to her: intense with one ('My dear, such divine music! I could have thrown myself at his feet'); *mondaine* with another; coquettish, or frivo-lous, or *sympathique,* as the occasion required. One could guess the latest company she had kept, for she had a great capacity for catching the tricks and tones of voice of other people. What Julia asked of people was that they should be distinguished in one way or another, even if it were only for chic, and perhaps it is under-standable that she should have wished to keep Aunt Essie out of her carefully collected parties, where everyone talked the same language, and each could be counted upon to draw the other out, to be amusing and sophisticated.

As a child, I was dimly aware of the two worlds, on one of which my father had turned his back. The one to which I belonged survived in Aunt Essie's little house.

She had a thin, rather long face, that somehow reminded one of a very delicate pitcher with the marks of the potter's thumb upon it in the faint hollows of cheeks and temples. With her dark gray eyes and pale gold hair, she must have been very appealing as a young girl; and when, years later than the time of which I am writing, I saw that colouring in a picture by my favourite painter, it seemed like a miracle that someone so many centuries ago should have put together such hair and such eyes and should have chosen a dove-grey drapery for the hood. It came to me with a further shock of surprise that my favourite painter would have been enchanted by my aunt, the only creature I had ever come across who repeated in her person the characteristics of his Virgin.

Aunt Essie was fond of grey, with cuffs and fichus and things of old lace. I knew her bits of jewellery by heart, and the stories attached to them. They were so much a part of her that they seemed to have absorbed something of her personality. Not only that, they shone with the flame of their respective legends, so that when the carbuncle heart winked on her breast, it was as if a spark of the marchesa's temper were imprisoned there; and the jade bracelet with the splinters of precious stones embedded in it called to mind the Chinese philosopher who had once shared a carriage on a P.L.M. express with her (she had been a great traveller on the cheap).

'Imagine my surprise when, having settled myself for the night—taken off my shoes, you know, and put my pillow in a comfortable position, congratulating myself on having a whole compartment to myself—the train stopped at Dijon, or one of those places ... I think Dijon, because I know I thought of roses and imagined them climbing up old grey walls ... I almost smelled them. ... Well, the train stopped at Dijon, and the station was muffled in darkness, just a dim glow from the buffet, and someone clanking along tapping the line, when suddenly there was a scuffle of suitcases in the corridor and someone pushed aside my door. The light was hooded and I couldn't see very well. "I hope," I thought, "my eyes deceive me, and it isn't an Oriental I am to be closeted with for the night." Not, Emmy, that I particularly cherished the thought of a European, either.

'My gentleman switched on the light, and—lo and behold—it *was* an Oriental, with a neat golden face and almond eyes. But there was something dignified and impassive about him. He wore a black cloak, and a kind of dry refreshing scent like chrysanthemums mixed with cedarwood came from it. "Excuse me," he said in French. "It was dark and I did not see that there was a lady alone here. Would you prefer, perhaps, that I remove myself to another carriage?" Not to be outdone in politeness, I murmured something about not minding at all, and shut my eyes. He rustled about a little, then pulled the shade over his light, and I went to sleep.

'But somewhere towards the small hours we were awakened by the ticket collector, and by that time I was so hungry I took out my thermos and sandwiches, and he opened a box and cut a slice of—what do you think?—*slab cake*, the last thing one would want to eat in the small hours. Suddenly he said, "If you will spare me a piece of cheese, I will give you a slice of cake. I am very fond of cheese." And that's how we got into conversation.

'I think, Emmy, we talked about everything in Heaven and Earth—all the abstractions that is, because he was a philosopher, and ideas were the breath of life to him—though he did like cheese.' She laughed in her bubbling infectious way. 'It was a very ethereal conversation, but I thought of material things, too: the scent of a tea chest lined with silver foil, and fairy tales printed on rice paper, and lovely embroidered buds and dragons and bamboo.

'When we got to Bourges, it was dawn. The green hills looked so fresh and peaceful, and there was a yellowish tinge on the church. He got down a suitcase and groped about in it, and suddenly put into my hand this bracelet. I couldn't say no. It would have been a sin against friendship.

'But the story has a very amusing ending. Two years later, I was taken to a reception at the British Embassy in Paris by a rather grand friend of mine, and who should be there but my Chinese friend! He knew me at once, though I must have looked very different in the Paris frock I had borrowed. He came across the room to me and held out his hand. "How do you do, Miss Cheese!" he said.'

Aunt Essie's friends, I thought, were different from other people. They had a queerness and a vitality that were transmitted to the presents they gave her. I have never met them, but, like beloved characters in a book, they were more real to me than the people I knew. Only Aunt Essie herself had the same quality of reality, of having a dyed-in-the-wool personality, of being herself right through to her bones. Who but Aunt Essie would have carried back from some rocky holiday a lump of quartz, or planted osiers for the sake of their red and gold wands?

When I was sixteen and had arrived at the uneasy stage of dim realization that love was not the entirely spiritual thing I had imagined, I felt my world shifting under my feet. So that was the secret shared by all grown-ups! But *Aunt Essie* couldn't know. There was nothing about her to suggest the possession of such dark knowledge. She hadn't married. No wonder, I thought!

There was no one I could talk to. Jane, my sister, was older than I, but perhaps she didn't know. I didn't want her life overshadowed, too. And Julia was out of the question.

But it was Aunt Essie, after all, who came to the rescue.

One day she happened to say about an old chair of pearwood that I had always loved, 'You shall have that for a wedding present.'

'I am never going to get married,' I answered dourly.

'Oh, aren't you? It's early days to make up your mind,' she said lightly.

'Aunt Essie, why have you never——?' I asked desperately.

'Perhaps because I like being a queen in my own right,' she said, with her little giggle, 'and a consort would have made hay of my little kingdom—not to mention children. They expect one just to be a mother. They resent one's friends, and look over one's correspondence without so much as a by-your-leave. They deny one a separate self. Besides, whom could I have trusted to be their father?'

'I don't know,' said I gloomily. 'There couldn't be anyone fastidious enough for you.'

'Now, Emmy, why this pessimism? You know in some ways I am a very frivolous woman. Oh, yes, I am. Your mother and I used to have terrible fits of giggles, and the crosser people got ("people" I suspected, meant my father), the more we laughed. You see, the same things struck us as quite irresistible, and we couldn't explain because nobody else saw that they were funny at all. Oh, Emmy, how I miss her! She knew that life can be terribly sad and utterly ridiculous, sometimes at the same moment.'

'Everything's so—so horrid,' I said, and burst into tears.

'My darling, what is it?'

'Love—it isn't beautiful at all. It's hateful.'

'So that's it.'

She set to work to treat the subject first from a scientific point of view, very cool and antiseptic. And then, with a spiritual legerdemain, she tossed it up to the sky and caught it again sprinkled with star-dust.

'And what about lovers and poets? Stars and nightingales and harps in the air. That's how they feel about it. When you fall in love, Emmy, you'll know.'

'So you did know. And you could go on behaving as if everything was as it seems to be,' I said.

She looked at me quizzically for a moment and seemed to be pondering some question, and then, throwing back her head as if she had arrived at a decision, she said, 'I'll tell you something I've never told a soul. When I was about five years older than you are now, and that was a long time ago, I fell in love. And it was—all poetry,' she added, in a hushed religious sort of voice.

'But you didn't get married,' I said.

'No. I didn't get *married*,' Aunt Essie replied, with a faraway look. 'He had a wife, you see.'

'Aunt Essie!' I said, shocked. 'I didn't think you could be so wicked. To fall in love with a married man!'

'But he didn't live with his wife. She had run away. Not,' she added hurriedly, 'that it is a wise proceeding to fall in love with men whose wives have left them. Much better not.'

'Couldn't he have got a divorce, and then you could have married him?'

'But the odd thing was that I didn't *want* to marry him. I was in dread, you see, of my poetry's dwindling into prose. An ordinary person, I thought, would be much better for prose. Not someone so wonderful. He was angry,' she said with a sigh, 'and that was the end of that.'

I considered Aunt Essie, and a dim notion of what my father and Julia found exasperating about her came into my head. She had a divine poetical silliness. Young as I was, I could see that. Years afterwards I realized that she had a Shelleyean disregard for ordinary human values and that her own set of values was too ineffable to be tolerated by people with both feet on the ground.

But I was strangely comforted. It was enough that Aunt Essie knew and was still her fastidious self.

It was a few weeks after this conversation that my father announced the visit of a distinguished playwright for the week-end. He had met Mr. Ellam several times at his club and had invited him down, ostensibly to see his collection of modern French pictures, but really because Julia had expressed a desire to meet him.

Julia flung up her hands in dismay. 'But Essie's coming to dinner on Saturday. We'll have to put her off.'

'Julia,' I said, desperately putting in my oar, 'you've put her off twice already. She'll begin to smell a rat.'

'I can't help that,' said Julia. 'I'm dying to meet Ellam. Essie's impossible. She just *can't* come, that's all.'

'Oh, nonsense!' said my father, for once. 'You can't treat the poor girl like that. She won't bother Ellam. We'll get Emmy to take her off your hands. You'll have to cajole her up to the school-room, Emmy, for a game of draughts, or to play duets. How would that do, eh?' cocking an eyebrow at me.

'I think it's a damn shame!' I broke out, throwing discretion to the winds. 'There's a damn lot more in Aunt Essie than you've ever guessed. She's worth a dozen blasted old Ellams or whatever they are. Damn, damn, damn!' I screamed, my pent-up emotions bursting out in a flood of appalling wickedness, and breaking into hysterical sobs, I rushed from the room.

Mr. Ellam arrived by the afternoon train. My father met him and brought him back to the expectant house. Julia's house, like Julia herself, was always keyed up for a special occasion, though I doubt if a speck of extra polish was put on, for none was needed. No, it was more a question of some change in the arrangement of the furniture, some object of virtu that had been hidden in the background given a prominence, a Persian rug spread in an unaccustomed place, a picture changed, and of course a greater profusion of flowers; as if Julia, standing back and looking at familiar things, had seen in them new potentialities, as if her own perceptions had been quickened by her preconceived idea of her visitor's.

Certainly the Pissarro, with its curdled snow, blue shadows, and swirl of gold from a lighted window, looked delicious in the hall over the Spanish coffer that had been brought out of obscurity to glow in the afternoon light. On the coffer, and just under the picture, was a green bowl filled with white roses. 'Lovely, lovely!' I said aloud, but with an obscure jealousy in my heart. A person with such very black eyes as Julia's to see such delicate colours, to make such exquisite juxtapositions! And all for old Ellam—that snob, who was considered too grand to meet Aunt Essie.

If they could but know of the Chinese philosopher! Chinese civilization was the oldest in the world. As for the subtlety of that race, it was a byword. A mere Englishman, a mere playwright, couldn't begin to fathom its depths. And he had talked to Aunt Essie for hours. He had called her *Miss Cheese!* There was the jade bracelet like a trophy brought back from fairyland, to prove the reality of that excursion into the realms of romance—but a romance far above the commonplace conception of something mixed up with the scent of orange blossom and the sound of wedding bells. The dry delicate fragrance of chrysanthemums and a friendship as rare as some unique Tang horse, an experience so ineffable that romance was a crude and tawdry word to describe it—that was something of which the Ellams and the Julias had no conception.

And the real lover, who was too wonderful to be married to!

People like Julia could never have made such a poetical renuncia-
tion. No one would ever be too wonderful for Julia to grab. The
more wonderful, the more she would snatch. She wouldn't have
hesitated to ask *Shelley* to dinner and show him off to her worldly
friends; except that it would have been Byron she'd have been
after in those days.

I made up my mind to look down my nose when I had to go
into the drawing-room. They wouldn't notice, of course—Jane
and I might not have existed so far as Julia's friends were concerned—but it would be a private satisfaction. I owed it to my
rare, precious Aunt Essie to manifest my inward disdain as outwardly as I dared. I would be very silent and aloof, and hate them
assiduously in my heart all the time. I would say, 'No, thank you',
in the iciest voice to the most sugary cakes, and even if Julia were
too much preoccupied to remark on so unusual an abstention,
I should have the secret consolation of knowing that a heroic
gesture had been made.

'Here goes!' I said, making a face outside the closed door at
the gentleman I visualized on the other side of it, in morning
coat, striped trousers, and, very likely, with a carnation in his buttonhole; a man-about-town such as one saw in St. James's Street
on one's rare visits to London, who had what one imagined were
ducal manners. But who also had a terrible twinkling condescension to schoolgirls, which made them feel miserably silly and
tongue-tied.

But on opening the door, I had a shock. Mr. Ellam was so
utterly different from what I had expected. I saw a great shaggy
man in cinnamon tweeds, with untidy red hair and bushy eyebrows. He was screwing up his eyes and looking at Julia with a
gentle kind of smile, the kind of smile with which a noble giant
might regard some delicate creature of another species.

'My daughter, Emily,' said my father, as I hesitated in the vicin-
ity of the giant, with a hand that had been outstretched and then
withdrawn and now quivered uncertainly by my side.

I knew directly I put my hand into Mr. Ellam's that I could
never look down my nose at him. It was as if he could feel my
pulse fluttering like a bird in his fingers, and was counting its
beats to find out about my heart.

'Have you read *In the Palace of the King*? No? It is a book you will like, I think. I'll send it to you,' he said.

It was as if his curious pale blue eyes, looking into mine, had sought out and found the essential me, disregarding my pigtails and tunic and the label 'schoolgirl' mentally affixed to my person by every other man and woman I had ever met (except of course Aunt Essie). Gently he had made me aware of my interesting, different, immortal self. Delicious intoxication! No wonder I gave him my heart unreservedly, no wonder I fell in love at first sight with this lordly stranger, who, as if he were setting a crown on my head, had recognized me as a person in my own right, a *special* kind of person, one who would love a book that he himself found beautiful. I never doubted that, then; though of course he must have remembered what had delighted himself at sixteen. (It came, in due course, an old book with his own name on the flyleaf and a date of thirty years before. Underneath he had written: 'Emily Browne, from her friend, Mark Ellam. And thereto I plight my troth.' It was long my most cherished possession.)

'You know,' Julia said, dispensing tea, 'I look upon you as the English Chekhov. I like the haphazard way things happen in your plays, so like life, after all. And there is one character who always turns up, a subsidiary one, but really, I feel, the key to whatever it is you imply—but never *state*,' she added, in her soft, voluptuous voice, holding the cream jug poised above a cup while she sorted out her thoughts.

'Cream?' she said. 'And sugar? I expected you to like Russian tea, so there *is* lemon. Philippa in *The Staring Owl*,' she continued, 'who says that shattering thing over her shoulder as she goes up the stairs. It is that which sets the ball rolling, isn't it? And Margaret in *And This Our Life*, putting the spindleberries in the vase while the row is going on ... and the little governess who makes the sign of the Cross over the man asleep on the sofa.... The same woman, really, under her different guises. I feel that she is the real heroine. Am I right or not?'

'She has a way of creeping in,' Mr. Ellam said, *sotto voce*. His remark seemed to be an aside, as if he were not really answering my stepmother. Perhaps he had already heard this opinion expressed in another quarter, for Julia, that omnivorous reader of everything modern, seldom knew, I suppose, whether her ideas were really her own.

'One's characters take the law into their own hands,' he said, aloud, with his delightful smile.

'You certainly got off with old Ellam,' said Jane, when we were dismissed after tea to the schoolroom. 'He kept drawing you into the conversation as if you were a grown-up woman. Julia was quite peeved. Doesn't she just love to keep the talk highbrow? I wonder why he did it,' regarding me dispassionately. 'You aren't a quarter as pretty as me. I expect you remind him of his dead wife or something.'

I said nothing. A great gulf, I felt, yawned since the afternoon between Jane and me. How could she be so . . . common?

There had been no time to warn Aunt Essie that she was to meet so distinguished a person. Her glory, I am afraid, was a little dimmed for me. She was so incalculable. One didn't know at all how she would take Mr. Ellam. It might very well be that she would behave as if he were just anybody. She might air her views on some important topic, quite unconcerned about seeming peculiar—her odd unpopular views that diverted the conversation into unlooked-for channels or dried it up. How ardently I wished that Aunt Essie were not coming after all! And, in a way, it had been my doing. A wild idea of waylaying her in the hall and giving her a hint that he was a unique person and must be treated with great reverence came into my head.

I darted down in my shantung frock, with this end in view. But I was too late. Mr. Ellam had preceded me. I could see his red head over the banisters. He was slowly descending the next flight of stairs, and as I reached the first-floor landing, I heard Aunt Essie's voice in the hall dismissing the parlourmaid who had taken her cloak.

She had paused to sniff the white roses and consider the Pissarro, she was wearing pale grey chiffon, her one evening frock.

'Good God! Esther!' I heard Mr. Ellam say in the strangest voice. It was like a scene on the stage. Young as I was, I knew that the moment was charged with drama. I knew it from that whisper of his that was yet a cry. They were alone in the hall, with the light shining down on the faded gold of her hair and on the snow in the picture and the snow of the roses.

She stood very still and looked at him as one might look at an apparition; and I remember how her eyes suddenly shone like water when the moon comes up.

'Mark,' she said. 'Oh, my dear ... after all these years! So you married again, Mark! Her photograph was in some paper. Such a beautiful woman! I have seen all your plays. Lovely, lovely plays. But are you happy, Mark? Tell me you are happy.'

'You have haunted me like a ghost,' he said, and suddenly snatched her to him and held her against his breast.

I had the strangest feeling of incandescence, as if my body had got into the way of a falling star and had been dissolved into light, and it came to me with a shock that I had been eavesdropping and had heard what I had no right to hear. How unimaginably beautiful life was! I turned and fled back to my room.

Exalted with my secret, I couldn't imagine what the evening was going to be like, how those shining ones would comport themselves during the absurd process of dining ... and afterwards, in the drawing-room with my father and Julia.

But when I went, tremulously, into the drawing-room, Aunt Essie wasn't there. Mr. Ellam, with a glass of sherry in his hand, was talking about the Test Match, of all things, to my father, and Julia was smoking a cigarette and blowing the smoke into little rings. She was wearing her diamond earrings and looked very beautiful.

Dinner was announced at once.

'But Miss Browne ... we'll have to wait a few minutes, Parker,' Julia said.

'I let Miss Browne in some time ago, ma'am. I think she must have gone away again,' remarked Parker.

'How very odd! My sister-in-law is an incalculable person. I suppose she changed her mind,' said Julia, turning to Mr. Ellam. 'But perhaps it's just as well. I don't think, somehow, she is *quite* your cup of tea.' She smiled her little mischievous, bewitching smile.

The queer thing was that Mr. Ellam didn't say a word.

But his silence sounded so loudly in my ears, it was like the bang of a door in Julia's face. Oh, glory! Now I knew who had a way of creeping into his plays, who'd always be there.

'Come,' said Julia, all unconscious, leading the way with an air of triumph. As we followed her, Mr. Ellam slipped my arm in his and pressed it gently against his side. It was almost as if, in some strange way, he knew that my young heart was ready to burst.